Teaching Machines
how To Cry

Teaching Machines how To Cry

Paula Hidalgo-Sanchis, phD

ISBN: 978-989-35309-0-0

This is a work of fiction. Names, characters, places, and incidents either are the product of the author's imagination or are used fictitiously. Any resemblance to actual persons, living or dead, events, or locales is entirely coincidental.

First Edition: 2023
Published by: Paula Hidalgo Sanchis
www.paulahidalgosanchis.com
contact@paulahidalgosanchis.com

Cover and book design by Paula Hidalgo Sanchis
Edited by Laura Ellen Joyce
Author's photo by BH Photo

Contents

To Ran and her nine daughters

With thanks to my sons, Noah and Alan,
for inspiring me every day

PROLOGUE:
A QUESTION OF PROBABILITY

Porto, 2011.

This story begins with an attempted murder. Without it, the main events of the narrative would never have occurred. The attempted murder happened many years before our story begins, and it was part of the decision that led to the Hölfang Foundation concealing the specifics of its programs. The murder attempt was carried out by Mr. Austin. The relevance of which, you will come to see.

Mr. Austin was a reputable businessman, a loving father of three children, and a devoted husband to Ms. Austin. He was also a board member of the Hölfang Foundation, an institution that did applied research to advance the work of an international corporation that specialized in bionic AI technology: Hölfang Industries.

As Mr. Austin was highly esteemed by the other Foundation board members – when he was acquitted by a jury for the attempted murder of his mother-in-law, they were all pleased.

"There is proof that he was not in his right mind on the day of the events," one board member said.

"He clearly suffered prolonged psychological torture from his mother-in-law," another added.

"Yes, friends and relatives testified to that. He clearly had an emotional breakdown," chimed in a third.

Mr. Austin felt terribly sorry about his actions and after a prolonged period of sick leave, and therapeutic support, he regained his pleasant personality and went back to work.

By the time he re-assumed his role as board member at the Foundation, the human-Like-Machine program, known as hL-M-p, was in progress. This program was a flagship initiative to produce a new generation of machine workers. 'Machine workers' were what the Foundation called multi-purpose AI machines that did jobs that were done traditionally by people, for example health care assistants or warehouse operators.

E was the star of the hL-M-p. It was an advanced AI prototype, designed to aid patients living in nursing homes. E functioned as a hybrid between a nurse and a household appliance. Programmed to be kind, and nice, it was also strong as an ox, and able to carry people around. It was also very skilful in other ways, from being able to turn book pages, to performing blood pressure checks. E could even do the laundry. The AI prototype was happily accepted by patients, not least because of its bantering conversation style, and its dry British sense of humour. But while it was very likable, the one issue was that it could also be clumsy in spite of spending long hours in the gym training its motor skills.

Because of its clumsiness, E failed a lab test. During the disastrous test, E tripped over a puppet that stood in for a patient waiting for supper on a couch. The AI prototype was carrying the food on a tray when it stumbled over a coffee table and landed on the figurine which ended up covered in vegetable soup and partially smashed.

The team working at the hL-M-p commissioned an independent evaluation of the failed test. This evaluation concluded that E could hurt people unintentionally, and even commit involuntary manslaughter. To avoid this future scenario, teaching E not to harm humans became the hL-M program's priority.

As innovative ideas were needed to achieve the new program's goal, the Hölfang Foundation hired an enthusiastic team of experts to work on the task. The young and brilliant scientists decided that the best way to ensure that E would not harm people, was to teach it morals.

But 'what morals?' was the question they faced.

After long brainstorming sessions, they agreed the answer was to teach E the top ten ethical values most respected throughout human history. So, 'which were those?' was the next question. To answer it, the team resolved to do a case study.

With dynamic discussions and drawing many diagrams, the experts agreed that the scope of the case study would be human recorded history.

"After all, human beings were only evolved when knowledge was expressed in writing," the lead data scientist said. Accordingly, ancient history was discarded as irrelevant for the research.

Diving into humanity's written history, the team realized that some written records, such as Egyptian hieroglyphs, weren't easy to understand. To address this, they adjusted the scope of the case study with a new timeframe. The new timeframe was from 2,600 B.C. onwards. 2,600 B.C. was the date of a Sumerian cuneiform script that had been identified by historians as humanity's first intelligible written text.

Once the new timeframe for the study was set, the team combined and categorized humanity's written legacy dating back to 2,600 B.C. Hours and hours of work were spent on collecting all available data sources, including manuscripts, historical documents, court transcripts, magazines, poetry, philosophical essays, children's books, religious papers, song lyrics, novels, and newspapers.

Then, the scientists wrote several algorithms to do a cross-sectoral examination of livelihoods, political and societal structures, creative arts, religions, and educational systems in the texts. With computations, the team analyzed the data with scatter plots, the Pearson correlation coefficient, the correlation matrix, principal component analysis (PCA), and Lasso regression. But the computations didn't yield the expected results, and only weak correlations and causations were found among the data points.

The findings of the case study were irrefutable: a core set of ethical values that guided people to do right or wrong in the selected timeframe wasn't found. The team concluded that the reason was that 'human history is too inconsistent'.

To advance the implementation of the hL-M-p, a quality assurance team proposed that E would just have to learn the seventh commandment, 'thou shalt not kill'.

The new proposal was presented to the Foundation's board for approval. A vote was conducted. The tally was eleven votes in favor, and one against. Can you guess who that one vote came from? It was the unintentional criminal, Mr. Austin, who deeply regretted attempting to murder his mother-in-law but believed that manslaughter could be justified sometimes.

At the same time, as was the normal practice, the scientists who conducted the study on moral values published a paper with the proceedings. The paper was entitled: 'Teaching E to be good: a scientific approach', and it was published in the journal *Science Today*.

When the paper was disseminated, something unforeseen happened: many voices questioned the scientific rigor of the study. Social scientists voiced their concerns about the methods used. Historians challenged the timeframe of the case study. And anthropologists claimed that the scope of the study had missed the fact that Homo Sapiens, or the wise man, had walked the Earth for three-hundred-thousand-years.

In response to the criticism, the lead data scientist issued the following statement: 'It's not true that the history of humanity was simplified for the purpose of the study. The broad scientific community recognizes written knowledge as a turning point in the evolution of human intelligence. The combination of logograms and syllabaries in the selected Sumerian cuneiform script is considered by many to be humanity's first writing system. So, it is reasonable to use that readable text as the milestone that marks the beginning of the evolution of men. Humans were not evolved before they learnt how to write.'

His statement 'humans were not evolved before they learnt how to write' went viral and ignited more criticism. A renowned philosopher then said: 'The Hölfang Foundation has simplified the complexity of humankind to fit it into machine-learning reality.' After this, a media scandal developed.

For the first time since it was established, the Foundation was under public scrutiny. 'It's an unprecedented scandal', the chairman of the board said.

The 'unprecedented scandal' resulted in delays in the implementation of the hL-M-p. In addition, the costs increased by 27 percent due to additional expenditures on lawyers and marketing consultant fees.

To avoid further criticism, setbacks, and extra-budgetary expenditure, the board decreed that all research would be kept secret from then on. 'The world will still benefit from our work, but we'll not be interrupted again' the chairman stated. To implement this resolution, the Foundation's board approved a confidentiality policy that all employees should follow.

After further discussions, the board decided to suspend the hL-M-p indefinitely.

E was then re-programmed and deployed to work at the Foundation's warehouse, to operate a forklift. Its duties were, of course, limited to moving packages labelled as 'non-fragile'.

And this is not the end but the beginning of a story. A story full of AI prototypes and also human hope. Full of machine learning and life learning. A story, I think, and I feel, you will like.

EMPTY

Porto, February 01, 2033.

Alba sat in a reclining teak chair on her apartment terrace at 7:31 a.m. She wore her pyjamas, and was wrapped in a blanket, holding a mug of green tea with both hands. As she sipped her drink, she admired the immensity of the Atlantic Ocean. Then, turning her gaze to the charming Farol Da Nostra Senhora Da Luz, or 'Lighthouse of Our Lady of The Light', she was once again mesmerized by it. *What a peculiar place—why was I drawn to this place with the octagonal tower?*

The lighthouse had drawn the young woman to live in the neighborhood as it had previously guided boats to the shore. Alba had discovered it by chance when she had been house-hunting in the area. When she had found herself standing in front of the heart-shaped, forged iron gate that guarded the Farol's entrance, she immediately decided to live close by for no reason she could articulate. This had happened two months ago, just a few days after she had relocated to Porto, the Portuguese coastal city in the Northern Region where she had lived as a child.

Finishing her tea, she swiftly changed into her jogging clothes. At twenty-eight years old, she had a healthy and strong athletic body as a result of practicing different sports. She had never let her bionic leg stop her. She knew that was the first thing people noticed about her, but the second thing was her intense blue eyes. She shook off these thoughts as she prepared for the run. She enjoyed running these days. Sometimes she felt like she was running towards something, and other times, away from something else. From what she didn't know, and she tried not to think about it. She just enjoyed running. Especially in the early morning.

In thin thermal underwear, turquoise leggings, and matching sweatshirt, and a light down vest, she headed out to the beach walk. Climbing down the stairs in the apartment building, she pulled up her shoulder length light brown and messy hair into a high ponytail, placed her earbuds in her ears, and began a meditation playlist. The repetitive, calming sounds soothed her in the morning.

Stepping on to the boardwalk at the Praia da Luz, or the 'beach of the light', she had flashbacks of her childhood playing with her cousins at the long and sandy beaches in Gaia, the town across the river with Porto. She smiled, seeing the fine sand, the small rocky formations and the white foam of the waves that spread for many meters on the shore. *It smells like mussels here.* She began to run.

After forty-five-minutes of running, she was back home. *I really need to start unpacking,* she thought looking at the carton boxes lying around. *Next weekend. I'm so glad I found this place, it's fantastic to live so close to the beach.* Alba had settled in a studio apartment with an open plan living room, sleeping area, and kitchen. It had a large terrace that compensated for the tiny indoor area.

She ate a cereal bar, and, following a quick shower, she combed her hair, put on some discreet make-up, and opened the wardrobe.

What to wear? It's cloudy and drizzling today? Yes! No surprise there. And cold? Not too bad.

She chose an oversized beige wool dress with a brown leather belt, black blazer, and high black boots. Then, she checked her outfit in the wall mirror.

Beige is not the best for my skin color but with the black jacket I don't look that pale. This will look good with my red coat. Not too formal or too casual – just right for a think tank!

She poured another tea into a thermos cup and headed off to catch the bus.

*

As she waited, a thick sea fog suddenly surrounded her.

Sadness feels like fog. You don't know where it came from or where it goes, but you feel it inside. It expands from your chest to your legs, your arms, and your head, reaching every cell of your body. You can almost see the tiny water droplets inside you, but you cannot grasp them. You cannot touch the fog, but it is inside you, just as it is around you. When you feel sadness, a part of you makes you believe that your heart is too tired to feel. A voice tries to convince you that you are empty and that there is only fog inside you. You feel that all your desires, all your dreams, and all your expectations are taken away by the fog because you just can't hold them inside you.

The 500-bus arrived, and she sat by the window on the second level of the large autonomous vehicle. As she gazed outside, her internal monologue continued.

Sadness feels like wandering the streets of a residential suburb in Beijing without a destination and you find yourself lost. You do not know where to go, and you cannot ask for help because you don't speak the local language, and nobody speaks yours. When you are sad, you don't understand why people laugh. You can only stare at others laughing on the street, feeling empty inside. Then, you ask yourself the question 'will I ever laugh again?'.

Thick tears fell down her face now. Feeling them, she reacted and shook off the emotion.

What's wrong with me? I've got everything in life to feel happy. I'm young and healthy. I'm smart. I'm beautiful. I had a very good education. I'm starting a great new job today. I'm privileged! My parents love me, and I love them. I have friends. I just moved to Porto. Why can't I enjoy life like everyone else? Something is missing in my life, but what? I have saudades, that phrase is so beautiful in Portuguese for melancholy or longing, but saudades of what?

She was frustrated, thinking about that feeling of loss that had accompanied her since she could remember. She had grown up with it.

And despite the support of therapists, she couldn't find a reason for her saudades. Today, as she wiped her tears away, she realized that her longing had only grown stronger over time.

What is wrong with me? This morning I cried when I saw fog, and yesterday I cried when I was with friends instead of having fun. She remembered the evening before when she joined her childhood friend Leonela and other friends on a terrace by the Douro River. While the others chatted, watching the sun disappearing into the water, she had disconnected from the conversation, stared at the horizon, and begun to cry.

"What's wrong Alba? Are you alright?" Leonela had asked.

"Nothing, nothing – I'm fine. Sorry, I'll go now. I'll call you later," she had answered, before leaving.

Today, again, she tried, once more, to understand her emotions.

Sadness is just the emotion on the surface, a layer on top of gloominess, melancholy, and despair. No matter what I do or what I try, deep inside, I feel as if there is a hole in my chest. As if something very important was missing from my life. I'm so tired of feeling empty. I'm tired of not knowing what it is that I miss so much. Years of psychotherapy didn't help. I found no answers. I've tried to ignore it all my life, but I just can't.

When she arrived at the Mercado Ferreira Borges, or the Ferreira Borges Market, Alba got off the bus. Feeling the morning sun shining in Porto's old town, she felt better instantly.

Ah, this is much better. Come on, come on, I can do this! I can enjoy my first day at my new job. I've been given an incredible opportunity and I'm going to make the best of it.

She wiped her tears once more, retouched her makeup using a pocket mirror, and walked towards the Hölfang Foundation, determined to have a good first day at work. As she walked over the cobblestones of the old town, she instinctively touched her left leg, the one that was partially bionic. Then, by association, she thought briefly of her childhood companion, M. Though she had no time to dwell on this thought.

*

Without any trace of tears on her face, Alba stood in front of the old Palacio Da Bolsa, or the Stock Exchange Palace, which was now the headquarters of the Hölfang

Foundation. She entered the building through large wood and iron doors, passed a security post, and registered at the front desk.

As she waited for Ms. Vivian, the HR officer, in the central courtyard, she admired the elegant orthogonal metallic dome with glass panels. The lower parts were decorated with wooden frescos reproducing scenes of the Sistine Chapel and white marble with green veins. *This building is so impressive... the Hölfang Foundation's premises are in some of the most iconic historic sites of Porto in the Ribiera district: the Palacio da Bolsa, the Mercado Ferreira Borges, the Igreja and the Hospital de São Francisco, I wonder how they managed to do it...*

A lady with a gentle voice greeted her. "Good morning, Ms. Alba, I'm Ms. Vivian, your HR officer."

"Good morning, Ms. Vivian, pleasure to meet you. That's a nice blazer," she said, looking at the striking paisley-printed silk blazer with blue, and yellow tones.

"Oh, that's nice of you to say, thanks. It's vintage. This way, please, I'll give you an introductory briefing in my office. Ready for your first day?"

"Yes, I am."

Alba followed the HR officer climbing up a massive stone stairway and passing by high granite walls and ceilings adorned with antique chandeliers.

This place looks like a museum. If it wasn't for the neon lights contrasting with the stone walls, I would think I was in one. Wow, Ms. Vivian really has a style, she thought, looking at her silver hair arranged with victory rolls.

Ms. Vivian put her wrist in a reader on the doorframe and opened her office door. It was a small white room furnished with transparent acrylic furniture. The only touch of color was from the small dolls piled up on a shelf.

"My little collection of souvenirs from mission travel to the Foundation's offices and centers around the world. This is my latest acquisition, from our new office in Honolulu," she said holding a small doll delicately. Please sit."

"As you know well Ms. Alba, the Hölfang Foundation was established twenty-seven years ago by Hölfang Industries... The development of new prototypes particularly benefits from this setting..."

As Ms. Vivian talked, Alba, who had followed the Foundation's work over the years, nodded.

Ms. Vivian continued. "The Foundation has eight-hundred-and-ten employees as of today, counting you of course, with a ratio of ten percent locals and seventy percent internationals."

"And the other twenty percent?" Alba asked.

"The other twenty percent are our machine workers. You'll receive a briefing on them later in the week. The Instituto de Pensamento, or 'Thinking Institute', where you'll work is the Hölfang Foundation's affiliated think tank. The center does applied research, and advocacy, on issues related to bionics at the national, regional, and global levels. It's an international center of excellence, and a well-known actor in the policy arena. We are delighted to have you join the Instituto, Ms. Alba.”

Alba tried not to smile as she listened thinking that Ms. Vivian spoke a like bit like a programmed machine worker.

“All our employees are fitted with a Foundation microchip, she said, showing her wrist to Alba. “It has the standard functionalities of personal chips plus some nice extras. With it, you can access your authorized areas, make payments, withdraw research materials, access your work calendar and many other things. You'll get yours inserted at the operations branch. I'll walk you there now. After that, you'll go to the Instituto where a colleague will welcome you. Do you have any questions?”

“No, not at this time Ms. Vivian.”

“Of course, you don't need a briefing on Porto as our other international colleagues do, because this is your hometown. Are your parents happy with your relocation here Ms. Alba?”

“Yes, they are very happy indeed.”

*

After having the electronic chip inserted, Alba walked over to the Instituto de Pensamento. There, a large young woman greeted her under a stone Baroque portal.

“Alba! Good morning, welcome, welcome, my name is Isongo, Ms. Vivian asked me to wait for you here.”

“Good morning Isongo, nice to meet you.”

"Was she wearing one of her vintage pieces? She loves them."

"Yes, she was. A very nice jacket. Your dress is very nice as well," Alba said, smiling at Isongo who wore a dress made of African print waxed fabric.

"Thanks. I work as a junior researcher at the Instituto, the same as you and I'll give you the official welcome tour of the premises. So, this is the old Igreja de São Francisco, or Saint Francis's Church, if you prefer," she said turning and making a theatrical gesture with her arms.

"Lovely."

"Let's go! I'll show you around and I'll introduce you to the team. You've got your chip already, right? Always look for the reader at the security posts to access premises, just like this."

Inside the old, Gothic building, Isongo led Alba to a room lined with bookcases stacked with antique leather books. It also had a soft carpet, art deco sofas, and reading lamps.

"We start the briefing here. I need coffee!" Isongo said pressing a button on a sofa arm.

A machine worker arrived a few seconds later. Alba smiled seeing the short, rounded white machine worker that came with a sophisticated drinks cart on wheels.

"Latte with almond milk for me," Isongo asked putting her wrist next to a reader in the machine worker's arm.

"Green tea, please," Alba asked doing the same.

"So, are you new to Porto?" Isongo asked laying back on a purple velvet sofa.

"Oh, no. I grew up here."

"Really? You are one of the few locals in the team then, most of us come from different parts of the world. Whereabouts did you live in Porto?"

"The Fluvial neighborhood. It's like forty-five minutes' walk from here. My parents still live there."

"I know Fluvial. It's close to the river. Did you find a nice place in the same area to live now?"

"No, I've settled in the Foz neighborhood now at the mouth of the river. It's close to the ocean, and a half hour walk from my parents."

"Cool."

"And where are you from?"

"I'm from the DRC but studied and worked in Canada before I came here. Did you know of the Foundation before?"

"Yes. I participated in one of its programs when I was a child."

"Really? what program?"

"It was called eMotional-Machine?"

"Interesting name. I want to hear all about it. We've got time, we've got ninety minutes scheduled for your introduction, so we have time. Go on, tell me all about that program."

Alba liked her cheerful colleague.

"Where to start?"

"What did you have to do?"

"My family and I hosted M at home for some time."

"Who's M?"

"An AI prototype designed to care for patients with special needs, like children, the elderly, and people with disabilities."

"Why did your parents agree to host an AI prototype?"

"Because the Foundation made them a very good offer. They were offered a state-of-the-art bionic leg for me," Alba said lifting her dress and showing her bionic leg. "It also offered its maintenance for a lifetime, a generous education grant, and future employment opportunities for me. I guess my parents saw it as their chance to expand my choices in life, to give me the best health care, education, and employment possibilities. They are good parents. They always do the best they can for me."

"What do they do for a living?"

"My father works as a topographer. My mother worked as a teacher at a secondary school but is retired now."

"So, how was hosting M?"

"My mother says that it was very easy because I liked it from day one. She says it didn't interfere with the family's routines, and it babysat me. My father has to work abroad a lot and my mother was always exhausted from work, that's why she retired early, so they welcomed M as my nanny."

"How long was M with you?"

"A bit more than two years. I was six when it arrived."

"But what was the point of M living with you?"

"M learned from me."

"Learned how?"

"Basically, following me all day long like a shadow."

"It followed you at home?"

"At home and anywhere, also to school."

"To school?"

"Yes, the school also accepted the offer from the Foundation to host M. In exchange, it received a generous donation of IT equipment. M shadowed me but didn't interrupt the school routines. My classmates were delighted with M – I think everybody asked for an AI prototype for Christmas."

"But why was it learning from you? What was M learning from a child?"

"Emotions."

"From a child? How come?"

"At that time, programming AI technology able to reproduce human emotions, was considered the next frontier in AI."

"It still is, in a way."

"The idea was that M would learn from a single data source and a small dataset instead of from multiple data sources and large volumes of training data which was the traditional method in machine-learning."

"But why learn from a child?"

"Well, the Foundation decided that the single data source from which M would learn should be a child because children express emotions more naturally than adults."

"I agree with that."

"Me too. Research shows that emotions in adults are biased. One of the reasons is the intake of antidepressants, anxiolytics, and painkillers, all of them suppress natural feelings. Another reason is that the rational and physical memories stored in different parts of the brain influence the way emotions are processed. Also, because adults tend to suppress certain emotions, like anger or rage, because they are perceived as negative."

"That makes total sense. I understand the learning from a child thing, but why you?"

"I don't know. I was just selected as the best candidate to be in the program."

"That's something. You were lucky then."

"Yes, I was very lucky."

"What a fantastic opportunity you had! I wanna hear more. And you're such a great addition to the team here with your experience in that program. Let's go now. We need to keep moving. We have a meeting this morning, and I need to do the whole introduction thing before that one."

"Okay."

Isongo guided Alba through the building stopping to introduce her to colleagues. As she talked, Alba looked around trying to memorize names and places.

"The building is from the fourteen century, and it used to be a catholic church... this is the main server room, where the catacombs were... this is Roger, our head of IT... Robert, show Alba the tombs and the skulls... they're cool, aren't they? I'm joking... no need to show her today... Roger is fun... that is the statue of Saint Francis of Assisi, a very famous art piece, I don't like it though ... please meet Ms. Anastasia, our Public Relations Officer... she's not fun... check the gilded woodwork in columns and walls, the building is famous for it... I like it... Please meet our director Dr. Badeaux, not cool, I'm kidding, he's the best... these are the old chapels in the church that now are used as working stations... Capela do São João Batista (or Saint John the Baptist chapel, not that you need translation), Capela dos Reis Magos (which means the Three Wise Men chapel as you know) ..."

In front of the former main altar Isongo stopped. "Here, good spot, you wait here. The research team will be meeting in ten for a brainstorming session, I've got to run and do something before that. So nice meeting you. You don't talk much but you are cool, and I say so because I know cool as soon as I see it," she added as she ran off.

Alba stood in front of the altar pieces decorated in shiny Baroque gilt-edged woodwork waiting for her colleagues to arrive. Touching the tiny mark left in her arm by the insertion of the electronic chip, she thought of M again. *Where are you, my old friend? Are you still around? I hope you are, and I hope I'll find you. And when*

I find you, I hope to find what I'm longing. I'm tired of feeling fog inside me, so tired. I've tried everything to get rid of it, but I can't, it never really goes away. Nothing helps. No one helps.

She continued in silence, looking at the woodcarvings of leaves and flowers that covered the ceiling and the large pillars on the sides of the aisle.

I know I lost something around the time when you left, but I don't know what it is. I can't remember. I know it's crazy to think that you might be able to help me. I know you are just an AI prototype, but something insides me tells me you would. I just know you would. When I saw that photo of the Foundation's twenty-fifth anniversary, I think I saw you there, but who knows, it might be any other prototype. It's almost two years since that photo. I hope it was you and that you are still around. And I hope I can find you.

WATER

Porto, February 01, 2013.

Alba and M sat on the large granite stones of the river wall by the Foz, or mouth, of the Douro River. Alba talked non-stop while M listened as if it was counting every word she spoke.

"I so love it here. I love it, I love it. Don't you love it? I love looking at the boats... They move slowly, don't they? No, the fishing boats never move. Why don't they move? What are they doing there? Do they fish? How can they fish if they do not move? Ah... I love the colors in the water... so much. Why is the water pink here, M? Is it pink, or is it orange? I'm not sure... Ah, no, no, no... it's not the water. It's the sun in the water!" Alba said, and then burst into laughter. "Did you see that? It's the sun in the water! Is it going to stay there? You think?" she asked, mesmerized.

Alba had been asking her parents' permission to go out alone with M for a long time. When she turned eight last week and was granted permission, she had planned this visit to watch the sunset by the river's Foz. When her parents asked why she wanted to go there, she had responded, 'Because it's my favorite place on Earth, and because I love water and sunsets, and the orange color in the sky. And because there, it is as if the water of the river and the water of the ocean dance together."

Now, as M placed a pink cloak gently over Alba's shoulders and fastened the neck button, she smiled at her companion.

"I'm not cold M but thank you."

"The atmospheric temperature will continue dropping fast at this time," M said.

Alba rolled her eyes. Then, looking at the water again, she continued talking. "It gives me peace in my heart to look at the colors in the water. My heart is happy. They are so beautiful. I feel as if a light switches on inside me… here… Is the heart here?" she asked pointing her sternum. "M, are you happy because I brought you here? We are coming back tomorrow," she said as she admired the pink and orange streaks in the sky.

"M? Did you hear what I said?" she asked.

"Yes."

I like M, but M doesn't talk much. I like that it is black and shiny though, so shiny. Not very tall, like me, a bit taller than me. And it looks like is wearing an armor and a helmet. It's beautiful… I like it.

Though her parents had explained to her the reason why M lived with them many times, she didn't understand it fully. But she didn't care. She had enjoyed its company from day one and she regarded M as something in between a best friend and a pet. She thought that it was too silent most of the time, but even so, she cherished it, as she cherished all that she found beautiful. *Beauty lifts my heart*, she thought. She had heard that expression in a movie and liked using it.

"Oh, the sun is almost gone into the water now, time to go. I'm hungry, and I'm cold," she said, suddenly. "I want to go home now," she added, looking at the boats. As she stood up, M followed her.

M said, "According to my calculations, the walk back will take 11 minutes, 38 seconds, 290 milliseconds, 47,371 microseconds, and 533,344.18 nanoseconds. The estimated time of arrival home is nineteen-thirty-one."

"And how do you know that M? You always talk as if you know everything."

"My prediction is based on your average walking speed in the evenings during the last month."

"And what about you? How fast do you walk?"

"I adjust my pace to yours."

Alba rolled her eyes again.

She wanted to prove M wrong, so she tried to walk fast, but after a few minutes, she slowed down. Climbing the steps at Rainha Dona Leonor Street, she stopped. Her left leg was more painful than usual. Caressing it, she asked for help. "M!!!! Please, help!!!!" she shouted, though her companion was just half a meter behind her. "I don't know what's wrong with my leg. I have a lot of pain today, M."

"Sorry to hear you are not feeling well."

The girl leaned on her companion, and in this way, they arrived home.

*

As she entered home, Alba felt better instantly. She liked her home. She liked that she could run from the entrance to the living room. She also liked the large table in the dining room where she sat to color, and her bedroom that had blue walls painted with starfish. Because her leg hurt when she climbed the stairs up and down, she spent more time on the ground floor, at the small table kitchen and in the living room where she had many toys. She also liked the pantry where she always found yummy things to eat for dessert. And she appreciated that there were always fresh flowers on the tables and in the bathrooms.

Seeing her mom, she forgot about the pain in her leg. "Mommy, can I watch cartoons today, can I?" she asked.

"Hi sweetheart," her mom said from behind a pile of books and papers. "Come here, give me a hug. How was the walk with M? Did you enjoy? No, you can't watch cartoons today, today isn't Wednesday. Cartoon day is Wednesday. Go and play now – I'm almost done with these math tests."

"Okay... M, let's play a game! Mommy says no cartoons today. Let's play the 'guess what this is' game. I'm going to score a lot today!"

"What's the 'guess what this is game'?" her mom asked.

"M is full of gadgets that can measure almost everything, Mommy, well, almost everything! In the game I guess what is what. It's a bit difficult because some words I don't understand, and also some of the things I don't understand very well. M explained many things to me but it's a bit difficult. But don't tell M or it is going to explain them to me again and it's soooo boring! I wanna guess. Last time I scored only two. There are many many things to guess and today I'm going to score a lot. Do you wanna play? Do you wanna see me play?"

"Oh, I understand, so M points at each of its sensors and then you guess what it is for, right? I can't play sweetheart, I've got to finish this pile of tests today, but you go ahead, I'll watch you play from here."

"M! mommy is watching me play, let's start. You point and I guess."

Alba sat on a cushion floor in front of M and stared at it concentrating. As the AI prototype pointed at a thin metal plate with metallic bars located over its right shoulder, she almost spoke, but she waited for her friend to ask first.

"What is this one for?"

"Rain."

"Wrong. Humidity."

"What is this one for?" M asked pointing at a membrane on its palm.

"Touch."

"Wrong. Pressure."

Alba put her fingers by her temples to concentrate harder.

"What is this one for?"

"Temperature."

"Correct."

"Yes!"

"What is this one for?"

"Position."

"Wrong. Proximity. What is this one for?"

"Light."

"Correct."

"Yes!"

"What is this one for?"

"Pressure."

"Wrong. Vibration. What is this one for?"

"Touch."

"Correct."

"I got three, I got three!" Alba said.

"What is this one for?"

"Color."

"Wrong. Infrared. What is this one for?"

"Sound."

"Correct."

"La, la, la, la, la, four, four, four! Mommy, four!"

"What is this one for?"

"Smoke."

"Wrong. Magnetism. What is this one for?"

"Tilt."

"Wrong. Level. What is this one for?"

"Weight."

"Wrong. Strain. What is this one for?"

"Soil moisture."

"Wrong. Liquid flow and level. Finish."

"How many? How many? How many did I score?"

"Four."

"Four, four, four, I scored four. Mommy, I scored for!"

"Very good, sweetheart. Now go and have a bath while I finish here, your dad will be home soon, and you can play with him before dinner."

*

At the dinner table, with a mouthful of spaghetti Bolognese, Alba listened to her parents talking about work and about organizing a family lunch with a lot of aunts, ancles and cousins. As she listened, she followed with a finger the blue stripes of the cotton tablecloth. Then, she touched the line of the level of the water in her glass, and then, she touched her mom's. Noting that her own glass was shorter that her mom's, she wondered how much less water she had. Then she compared the size of her fork with the size of her dad's fork and noted

31

that they were the same. She noticed then that the napkins matched the tablecloth and then read her name written on the white napkin holder. Then, she watched M watching her.

M is always clean. I get dirty playing outside, but M doesn't. Mom also doesn't. M never eats.

"Mom, what does M eat?" she asked, interrupting her parent's conversation.

"M has batteries sweetheart."

Like my race car.

"Yes, but Dad, why doesn't M have clothes? It looks like is wearing an armor and a helmet on the head but has no clothes, why hasn't it got clothes? M also makes a funny noise walking, like 'vuuptz, vuuptz'. Tell me again the story about how M came to live with us."

"M doesn't need clothes, teddy bear. And yes, I can tell you the story of why M lives with us again."

I like it when Dad is home for dinner. I don't like it when he travels for work. I don't like it when he's not home. But I like it when he brings me a present. Like the sugar cake he brought last time from an island.

"M was created at the Hölfang Foundation," her father said.

"Holfaaang... I can't pronounce it, it's too difficult."

"Hölfang Foundation, you went to the Foundation to do some tests, remember?"

"Yes, but why does M live with us?"

"We are participating in the eMotional-Machine program, teddy bear. M lives with us to learn from you."

"How come M needs to learn from me?"

"M is learning to take better care of people."

"What people?"

"People with special needs."

"Like cousin Antonio? Everybody says he has special needs."

"Yes, like your cousin Antonio."

"To learn what?"

"Emotions."

"Um?"

"Like excitement, anxiety, sadness..."

"M, do you want me to teach you how to cry? I'll teach you how to cry. You're funny."

"M, no need to answer that. Alba, now, eat your broccoli, you can teach M how to cry later."

"Okay, okay, but can I have ice-cream, pleeeeeeease? Mom?"

I want ice-cream and I like M very much. I'll teach M how to cry, I can do that; she thought as she left the dinner table and went to her play corner in the living room.

*

With a full belly, she had a bath, put on her pink pyjamas with white owls printed on them, and went to bed carrying her favorite stuffed animal, an extra-large dolphin, under her arm.

"Do you think that someone lives up there, M?" she asked, pointing out to the window with her right index finger.

"Your question is not clear to me."

"M, you do not understand sooooo many things… ALL THE TIME… I'm asking if you think that someone lives up there. Up there in the stars, like there there. Here, come here," she said, pulling the machine by the arm.

"Look, M, look. You follow my finger and then you draw a straight line, and then you continue all the way up, up, up, then when you see that star, then you stop. There. I really like that star. Do you think anyone lives there? Do you think that is cold there? I am a little cold now," she said, covering her head with the blanket.

In a few seconds, M reviewed all scientific papers, blogs, and books available about life outside of Earth.

"The first references to life outside of Earth appeared in—"

"Tell me a story, M," she asked coming out of the blanket. "The story of the unicorn that cannot find the magical forest, I love that story. Mommy tells me that story all the time, pleeeease M, please. No, no, tell me the story about how I'm special and because of that I was selected to be in the mmm something something program."

"Where do I start?"

"From the beginning."

"I came to live with your family because of you."

"That's so nice, that's why I like the story. Go on, tell me more."

"The Hölfang Foundation was seeking a teacher for me…"

"Why didn't they send you to school?"

"It's different for machines than for children. There are no schools for machines."

"There should be! You'll like it, I think. I like my school. Very much."

"To find me a teacher, scientists at the Foundation selected you among millions of children."

"Millions? I don't think so. Maybe they told you that but that's a lot. I don't think so."

"Yes, millions."

"And how they did they find me among 'millions'?"

"A team first reviewed the digital records of millions of children."

"The what?"

"The digital records."

"I don't understand."

"It means data on many things, for example your heartrate when you were a baby in your mom's womb, your favourite ice cream toppings, your medical records, the results of your IQ tests, your handwriting, your school reports, the movies you watch, the songs you like…"

"Okay, okay, a lot of things. But how do they even know this? Are you inventing this, M?"

"No. I've been trained on the basics of the eMotional-Machine program."

"I'm not sure I believe you – how do those scientists know what ice-cream topping I like? Do you even know what ice-cream topping I like?"

"You like sprinkles."

"Yes. Okay, you know, how do they know?"

"The Foundation has agreements with thousands of public institutions and private companies so scientists can access identifiable digital data for research purposes."

"For what?"

"For research purposes."

"The what? That I don't understand. M, you're supposed to be telling me a story, but you speak in a way that I don't understand. How did they find me? You have to speak more clearly, M."

"The team shortlisted hundreds of children based on the analysis of personality traits and proxies of behavioral patterns. These were subjected to a psychological profiling conducted by algorithms that analyzed art pieces as well as your voice tones and word choices in different life situations. Finally, a select few children undertook several in-person medical, biomonitoring, and human motion tests at the Foundation's premises."

"The what what?"

"You went to do some tests to the Hölfang Foundation. In those tests doctors and scientists asked you questions."

"Yes, I remember, it was looooong and boooooring. But I got a lollipop after each test, I got like six or seven, that was nice."

"You were selected by a rigorous scientific selection process."

"By a what... It doesn't matter, you just don't know how to speak to children."

"You were selected."

"Yes, but why me? I'm a bit faulty, you know? Mom and Dad say I'll need a new leg because my left leg is dying."

"You met all the program's requirements, including having a physical impairment. Years ago, you presented symptoms of a rare type of atherosclerosis that provoked a peripheral artery disease on your left leg. The disease is causing irreversible damage in the blood vessels supplying your limb. Your leg doesn't receive enough oxygen, and as a result, it's dying. Soon, it'll be amputated and replaced with an artificial limb."

"I don't want my leg to die!" Alba said crying. "I don't want to, I don't want to, call my mommy please. I want my mommy."

Alba's mom came to the room to soothe her daughter and told her the story of the unicorn. Listening to the story, Alba watched M observing her silently, seated on her bedside chair.

M is not mean, it's just not that good at saying things sometimes. And it takes care of me at night in case I'm not well because of my leg.

"Mommy, did you know that M knows everything that happens inside my body? M, you tell Mommy how."

"The miniature wireless sensors embedded in the bracelet and a pendant that Alba wears transmit her vitals constantly. I monitor her body temperature, pulse rate, blood pressure, and breathing rates twenty-four seven with a telemetry system."

"Yes, I know. Alba, time to sleep now," her mom said caressing her hair.

Calmed after receiving a lot of cuddles, hugs, and whispers, she fell asleep holding one of her mom's hands against her face.

*

As Alba dozed, she was, like every night, lulled to sleep by the sound of a song from another world.

'Waves, waves, waves of blue,

coming and going in a dance with you...'

Tonight, as every night, she felt as if the song transported her to a beach she didn't recognize. There, listening to the song, she felt Her. She couldn't see Her, but Alba knew She was calling for her.

Though Alba could not recognize Her, she felt safe in Her presence. She felt protected by Her, as if She was her guardian.

Tonight, as every night, Alba felt Her at the beach, waiting for her, calling her. With the song, She was showing her the way to find Her.

'Waves, waves, waves of blue…

… coming and going to a dance with you.

Despair and joy, rage, and compassion,

crashing and going in a dance with you.

Waves, waves, waves of blue,

coming and going in a dance with you.

Grief and desire, hope and bliss,

crashing and going in a dance with you.

Waves, waves, waves of blue,

coming and going in a dance with you.

Flooding and chaos in the order of things.

Tearing of time…

in a wave…

with you.

Waves, waves, waves of blue.'

WAVES OF BLUE

Porto, February 02, 2013.

"Morning," Alba said sleepily, waking up with the first rays of sun. "I had a dream, M. It was a strange dream because I felt I was awake. Do you dream a lot?"

As her companion approached the bed and stared at her, Alba asked, "What are you doing M?"

"I do not dream. I am measuring the length of the bed linen marks on your face."

Alba rolled her eyes and continued talking: "I had a strange dream. I'll tell you about it, but don't tell Mom and Dad, I don't want them to think that I'm weird because I've got weird dreams."

"I will not tell your parents about your dream, Alba."

"Promise?"

"I am not programmed to promise."

"Okay, okay," she said, rolling her eyes again.

"I was in the ocean. You know the ocean? I was standing on a big rock, but I was in the water, like far far in the water. I think as far as where they fish, not on the shore but really far. I like to swim close to the shore. It was strange to stand there, and I didn't get wet. That was strange because I was in the water, you know? And then, the waves and the winds were all around me, splashing, big splashing, around me. And I wasn't falling… That was strange also… There was, like, rain above me but more like spray from the ocean and the waves around me… And I wasn't scared… It was very strange. I wasn't falling, and I had no fear. I liked it there. It was like when you go to bed, you know? Like quiet. Like you. I felt like water. Ah ah ah, that is funny!" she exclaimed and then burst into laughter. "I love water. Don't you love water? You also love water, M, don't you? Don't you?"

"Water cleanses."

"But I don't remember the full dream, M. Something happened after the big waves, but I don't remember. It was very important though, that I know, but I don't remember. Don't tell Mom and Dad. Do you think I can have four cookies today?" she asked, jumping out of bed.

*

She washed her face with two fingers, brushed her teeth for a few seconds, and put on her school uniform – a sky-blue t-shirt, a grey skirt with grey socks, and a grey tracksuit jacket. Then, she rushed downstairs. After that, she left, carrying a ham and cheese sandwich in one hand and her school bag in the other and walked to the school bus stop with M.

Alba looked at the sandwich, disappointed. *I like Mondays. Mondays are 'cookie day'. My mommy gave me four last time but today isn't Monday.*

"So, M, you are supposed to be learning from me, what did you learn yesterday? How do you even learn?" she asked biting into the sandwich.

"I learn with a method called…"

"What's a method?"

"A method is the way of doing something."

"Okay."

"I learn with a method called 'deep learning'."

"Wait, wait, how do I learn? Do you know that?"

"At school, you learn with the Montessori method, which originated in Italy in the past century."

"Italy? Ummmm."

"You learn by making choices on which books to read, or where to play, among other things."

"I didn't know that."

"I learn with 'deep learning'."

"You also choose things?"

"No, I collect data from you, then I organize it into databases and label it. Afterwards, I look for patterns in the datasets."

"You collect data from me? How? How you do that? How dare you?" she asked bursting into laughter.

"I collect data through my sensors."

"Yes, I forgot, you told me that."

"I collect data through my sensors in the form of images, sound, measurements, and other formats. I organize the data into databases."

"Tell me one."

"One."

"No, silly, tell me one database. I don't know what that is. Hello? I'm only eight, remember?"

"Food_subject_A."

"What's subject A?"

"You are subject_A."

"Um? I don't understand."

"Subject_A is Alba. You."

"Why you call me that? You're funny. What data do you collect from me? Wait! Don't tell me your long blah blah blah that I don't understand. Examples, please."

"Last night, at dinner, I collected data."

"What data?"

"Time you spent eating, kilocalories you consumed per minute by food item, grams of food eaten and left on the plate, face and body expressions at the dinner table, and words you used in association with food items, such as 'disgusting' used for a white vegetable or 'yummy' for dessert. Also, topics of conversation and duration of silent periods. And the number of times you left the dinner table and what you did, for example picking up a toy from the floor."

"All that? that's a lot of work. And then what do you do with all that?"

"Upload the data into the database, review and clean it, correct empty fields and remove duplicates."

"And then?"

"Assign labels to it."

"And then?"

"The cleaned, organized, and annotated set comprised my 'training data'."

"M, you don't know how to speak to a kid. My teacher does. You need to learn that. I like my teachers very much."

When the bus arrived, Alba and M sat together.

"Okay, okay, you can continue telling me how you learn, go on."

"I look for patterns in the data collected."

"Patterns like in wooden blocks? That I understand."

"I look for patterns."

"How?"

"I build a complex artificial neural network, an ANN. ANNs mimic the human brain, and create a web of millions of nodes that emulate neurons. When they find a pattern, a node receives an input, and then sends out information as an output."

"I didn't get any of that. Tell me a pattern."

"When you ask a question that is preceded by one-hundred-and sixty-two words, built with nine consecutive sentences, and spoken with fewer breaths than average, the question is rhetorical."

"What's that?"

"You don't expect an answer."

"That's not true. I don't do that. Tell me another pattern."

"Pattern of bedtime behavior – you are in bed wearing pyjamas, you ask for a story, your mom tells you a story, you cuddle with your mom, then you go into non-REM sleep phase and then REM sleep phase."

"Oh. Tell me another pattern. A funny one."

"When you eat cauliflower, hake, or liver, you have a 'facial expression of disgust for food'."

"That's not funny, M. You need to learn about funny things. What is the opposite to a pattern?"

"An anomaly."

"Do you also find those?"

"Yes."

"Tel me an example."

"Last evening, looking at the sunset in the Foz. You talked about the colors in the water, and from 18:52 to 18:54 pm you had an abnormal level of glow in your eyes."

"What's abnormal?"

"Non-normal."

"I don't understand. But then, how do you know that I don't like cauliflower and not broccoli, they look alike, apart from the color."

"I label your data."

"You what?"

Alba looked through the window and started counting cars. She had gymnastics class at school today and the teacher had said that they would climb a rope and she wasn't sure she'll be able to do it. She didn't want anybody to say something about her leg again today. She liked it when M talked, though she couldn't understand most of what it was saying, it soothed her.

"Label data, the same way that your brain labels data. When you heard as a toddler, 'this is a ball', your brain added the label 'ball' to the rounded object."

"You're talking about balls now? What else?"

"When you said 'No, no, no,' cauliflower no. I don't like it. I don't want cauliflower. Can I leave it? I don't like cauliflower', I labelled your expression as 'facial expression of disgust for food'."

"I say what? go on."

"Then, I scan the meals_subject_A database, searching for data annotated with the label 'facial expression of disgust for food' and found several entries."

"Aha... And?"

"I build a simple model imitating the way your human brain makes sense of things. First, extract all the data points related to the facial expression identified and organize it in layers. Then, apply 'deep learning' and seek for correlations, causations, and associations among data points. Then, build a model, an algorithm. With it, I will predict a 'facial expression of disgust for food' next time you have to eat cauliflower, hake, or liver."

"Did you just say cauliflower? Is there cauliflower for lunch at school today? I don't like cauliflower. And I like most of my classmates, but not all, some say nasty things. Maybe today if I can't climb the rope they will."

Getting off the bus, feeling the sun in her face, she relaxed and asked, "M, do you know how many eyes flies have?"

*

"Mooooommmmmmy!" she shouted back home from school.

"It's good that we did not throw away the new sneakers' box last week. I need a shoe box, also maybe a milk box, or another box, you know, like a box box. I need them for next week. The teacher said that we are going to build a robot. Do we have a box, Mommy? Can you put it in my room? But do we have any box, Mommy? Do we have one at least?"

Before her mom could answer, she stormed in, dropping her school bag on the way and went to play in the living room.

"MMMMMM, MMMMM, come here, you! Look, look, look at this."

"Sweetheart, bring your bag to your room. Your cousins will be here soon. They'll stay for dinner today."

"M, Ana Inês and Lucas are coming! Come, look at this."

"Sweetheart, your bag."

"Yes, Mom!"

Alba didn't bring her school bag to her room because she forgot about it with the news of her cousins' visit. She also forgot that her day at school had been tough because she couldn't climb up the rope. After enjoying an evening playing and laughing over games and dinner, exhausted, she went to bed early.

In bed, she teased her companion, "M, what are you doing so quiet? You are always quiet."

"I'm not 'quiet' Alba. I speak when it is necessary."

"I'm teasing you. Good night, M. Wait, I'm going to teach you lesson one to learn how to cry. You want me to teach you how to cry?"

"Yes."

"Lesson one. You cry when you're very sad. Also, if you have like a lot of pain, a lot. And that's it. Wait, Dad told me once that if you are very, very happy you cry, but that I'm not sure, I'll ask Dad tomorrow. Yes?"

"Yes."

"But M," she said sitting in bed. "Today I couldn't climb up the rope, my leg hurt. I didn't cry. But why does my leg hurt so much this week?"

"You have a rare type of atherosclerosis that provoked a peripheral artery disease on your left leg. The disease is causing…"

"M don't tell me that my leg is dying again. I don't want to hear that."

"What do you want to hear?"

"That I'll be okay."

"You will be okay."

"Yes, but tell me why I'll be okay, how?"

"You will have surgery at the Hölfang Foundation's hospital, and you will receive a bionic leg."

"I don't want a bionic leg. I want a normal leg."

"Normal?"

"Yes, I want to be normal. I'm not, I have a leg that is not good, and I've got weird dreams. Normal people don't have weird dreams."

"Dreams are not logical."

"Yes, but will I be able to climb a rope with the bionic leg?"

"Yes."

"And play football a lot without pain?"

"Yes."

"Okay. And play tag a lot also?"

"Yes."

"But when do I have to go to the hospital?"

"The surgery is scheduled for next month."

"And is it cool to have a bionic leg? Will I be cool at least?"

"Cool?"

"Just say yes, M."

"Yes."

"Thank you. Good night, I'm tired."

"Good night."

Thinking about playing tag, she walked towards the land of dreams.

*

Where am I? I am lost. I do not know this place. Why did I come here? How? She looked around, confused, trying to see through the thick mist around. Nothing. She could only see darkness around. *What? I forgot where I must go. Where am I? Where am I going? I do not remember... Where am I? What is this place? I am supposed to go somewhere, but where? I am lost. I'm scared.* A chill in her spine made her want to run. But she couldn't. *I am freezing. It is so cold here, so cold.* With all her will, she moved one foot and then the other, and then she ran. She ran and ran feeling that her life depended on it.

As she ran, she heard a familiar voice in the far distance. "Nine hours, twenty-seven minutes, and eighteen seconds."

What? She focused on the voice and then heard it again, louder this time. "Nine hours, twenty-seven-minutes, and nine seconds. You need to get to the hospital."

Opening her eyes, she saw her shiny black friend in front of her.

"M? M? is that you? What? What is happening to me? I'm scared M. I don't want to die. You said I'll be okay, tell me M, what..." Then, she closed her eyes again.

DARK

Porto, February 03, 2013.

"Nine hours, twenty-five minutes, and…" M said entering in Alba's parents' bedroom interrupting their sleep.

"What? M? What happened?" Alba's father asked jumping out of bed.

"Nine hours…"

"What's the meaning of the numbers, M? Is this to do with Alba?" he asked.

"The time left before the bacterial infection spreads in the body."

"Bacterial infection? How is this possible? What happened, M?"

"I launched the replacement protocol."

"Darling, what is happening? Why is M in here? Is Alba all right?" Alba's mom asked getting out of bed.

"It's Alba. M is saying something about a protocol. Alba is in danger."

"M, what's happening?" Alba's mom asked.

"The drone ambulance's ETA is 02:43."

"ETA, what is that, M?"

"ETA: Estimated time of arrival."

"But how?" Alba's father asked.

"Where's Alba?" Alba's mom asked. They both ran to their daughter's room.

"Oh, she's so pale, and her pulse is so weak, this is bad. How long until the drone ambulance lands M?" Alba's mom asked.

By their side, M responded, "Eight minutes and..."

"Eight minutes darling," Alba's father said. "Is the Foundation's hospital ready for her, M? Is the medical team aware of the situation?"

"The hospital acknowledged the launch of the replacement protocol."

"Where is the ambulance? Why it's not here yet?" Alba's mom asked, crying.

"This wasn't supposed to happen. The surgery was planned in a month from now. M, tell us what happened," Alba's father said.

"She was in a deep REM dream phase with fast and irregular breathing, rapid eye movements, and slight twitching of her face..."

"She was sleeping, and?"

"Sensors detected a reduction in oxygen consumption combined with a low pulse and decreased body temperature. Visual exploration revealed a sudden paleness in her face and a skin ulcer in her left foot toe…"

"A skin ulcer?" the father asked checking the toe. "M is right, darling, look."

"Also, a swift decrease in the body temperature."

"Yes, she feels cold, oh, my baby girl," Alba's mom said.

"Symptoms indicate a severe blockage in the arteries, probably making the blood flow in the left leg to slow down. I launched the replacement protocol."

"That's good darling, that means that the medical team knows what is happening."

"What will happen when the ambulance arrives, M?" Alba's father asked.

"Her body is going into shock because of a bacterial infection. Shock must be treated first. The blockage in the arteries must be treated. Her chance of survival depends on the speed of the treatment."

"What are you saying M?" Alba's mother asked.

"Her chance of survival depends on the speed of the treatment. She might die."

"How much longer M? How much longer for the ambulance to land?"

"Six minutes…"

"It's going to be okay," Alba's father said, holding his wife's hand. "The medical team is waiting for her."

THE REPLACEMENT PROTOCOL

Porto. February 03, 2013.

Feeling dizzy and with heaviness in her body, Alba opened her eyes. "Mommy? Daddy?"

"Yes, teddy bear, we're here."

"Daddy, what happened?"

"You are at the hospital; all is good now. You had surgery last night."

"Surgery?"

"Yes, sweetheart."

"Where is M?"

"M is here with you. We are all here."

"Where am I?"

"At the Foundation's hospital. In the intensive care unit," her mother said caressing her hand.

Comforted with her mom's touch, she closed her eyes again. The bed was uncomfortable, the bedsheets felt like plastic, and she was scared of the cables attached to her head and chest. Ignoring it all and focused on her mom's hand, she dozed. After a while, awake again, she saw doctors and nurses coming and going, checking the cables without saying much. Then, she looked at the machines around that had blinking lines and made beeping sounds. "I don't like the smell" she whispered. "What's that smell?"

"Medicine and disinfectant, sweetheart."

"Why is the light on?" she asked. "Switch it off please, Daddy."

"I can't switch it off sweetheart, we are at a hospital, not home."

Resigned, she closed her eyes again.

A few hours later, she heard her parents talking. Too weak to speak to them, she just listened, half-sleeping.

"I'm so relieved, darling, so relieved," her mom said.

"I knew everything was going to be all right," her dad said.

"Everything went so fast, everything, from the ambulance she went straight into the OR."

"The head surgeon said that it wasn't really an emergency for his team because they had planned the entire procedure months ahead."

"I hope she won't be too traumatized by the amputation, what do you think?"

"We had the talks with her as the doctors advised... But we'll only know when she is aware of it. The doctors said that the surgery was smooth and without complications, that's what is important now. This hospital is one of the best in the world. Our daughter is in good hands here. Let's wait and see how she reacts, and we'll take it from there. An amputation is always traumatic," he said.

"You're right darling, we'll see when she wakes up. But what are you wearing? Are those your pyjama pants?"

"Yeah... With the rush, I only changed my top."

"Well, cotton grey sweatpants and light blue polo sweater, it looks similar to what you wear for your workouts..."

"This will make Alba laugh, she's awake, let's tell her."

"Mommy, Daddy... Can you tell them to switch off the light? I can't sleep. I don't like this hospital. I wanna go home, please. Can we go now, please?" she asked and then fell asleep again.

*

Porto, one week after the amputation

"Alba, have you noticed how soft this blanket is?" Her mom asked.

She touched the blanket a few times and made the effort to smile at her mom.

"It's soft."

The blanket is nice, and the bedsheets here don't feel like plastic. The fat white clouds painted on the walls are also nice.

"What's the smell here, Mom?"

"It's lavender, sweetheart, do you like it?"

"Yes."

"Am I going to stay here for long?"

"Yes, as I explained you yesterday, you are now recovering from your first surgery and waiting for the second. This is the recovery wing of the hospital."

"How long will I be here?"

"A few weeks."

"Weeks is too much. Can I go home now?"

"No sweetheart you can't go home. Yes, it's long, yes, but you need to recover from the amputation before you have your new leg."

"I don't want a new leg. I want my old leg. What am I going to do here for weeks?"

"A lot of people will help you recover here. There's going to be a doctor, a nurse, a pediatric psychologist, and a physical and an occupational therapist helping you."

"And M?"

"Yes, M also."

"And school?"

"A private teacher will come for you."

"A teacher just for me?"

"Yes, just for you, isn't that cool?"

"I don't know."

"How is the pain today?"

"It hurts."

"Now, what do you want to do this afternoon? Do you want to do some coloring?"

"No, I don't feel like. Later maybe."

"As you want. I have to go to work now sweetheart, you father will be here at lunchtime, and your aunt Albertina will come before he leaves. You can call me anytime, just ask M, all right?"

Alba looked at her mother who was wearing a mid-length, flowy dress with a round neck and puffed sleeves printed with blue and salmon colors. *I like puffy sleeves. I want a dress with puffy sleeves also.* Then she stared at the long beaded necklace with a matching bracelet that she was wearing. *My mommy is beautiful; I like her hair up in a top knot. My hair is like hers, light brown, and a little bit blonde. I love my mommy.*

When her mom left, Alba lifted the pink blanket and looked at her left leg that had been amputated below the knee area. She cried softly.

"I don't like it without my leg M, I don't like it. And the kids in school are going to laugh at me. Beatriz is going to say something ugly to me. She's not nice, Beatriz; she always says ugly things to other kids. One day she told Pedro that he was the f-word only because she doesn't like him. She's not nice. She's friends with Graciela, but she's not my friend because she's not nice. I don't want to go back to school without my leg. M, I don't want to go, I don't want to," she repeated, sobbing.

"You will not go back to school until you have a new leg," M said.

"Thank you, M, you're always nice." *I like M very much.*

*

Porto, one and a half months after the amputation.

On the way to the head's surgeon office, Alba complained to her father: "Why do I have to go? I don't want to."

"I know teddy bear, but the doctors said is important," her father said.

"I don't care, I don't want to go, I want to stay in the room with M and watch cartoons."

"You'll do that later, but now we're all going to learn about your next surgery, it's important for you to listen."

"Why?"

"I already explained you why Alba. The doctors say that it'll help you accepting the bionic limb."

"Your new leg sweetheart," her mom intervened. "The doctors say it's important for you to learn about the surgery."

"I don't want to."

"You can have a lollipop afterwards," her dad said.

"Two."

"All right, two," her mom said.

She liked the surgeon's office decorated with Asian-themed wallpaper and delicate porcelain figurines on display, but she didn't show that she liked it because she wanted everybody to know that she didn't want to be there.

Sitting quietly in a wheelchair, she played with a ball of blue tac while her parents sat at a red lacquer conference table and the doctor talked.

"As I explained to you when we first met, the prosthesis we'll attach to your daughter is a bionic leg. Allow me to remind you what this means," he said smiling at Alba. She didn't smile back.

The surgeon continued: "A bionic leg moves imitating the way a natural leg does. It's built with bionic technology that we use to create artificial systems with the characteristics of living ones. The bionic leg is a sophisticated version of a traditional prosthesis. As you well know, Hölfang Industries is a worldwide leader in the field so Alba will get a state-of-the-art piece."

Alba's saw her parents nodding as the surgeon spoke.

"As you know, the surgery will be implemented in five steps. I'll take you now to each of the steps. We'll have a Q&A session at the end, so I ask you to hold your questions until then."

He sounds like when my teacher explains math's, Alba thought.

The surgeon continued: "Step one will be the smooth manipulation of body tissue below the knee," he said, extending his right arm and showing his left thumb. "With this, we'll prepare the area to embed the artificial limb. "Step two," he said, also showing his index finger, "will mean an electrical device will be inserted into the leg. Step three, the bionic leg will be attached," he continued, lifting his middle finger. "And steps four and five," he added, showing all the fingers, "will be the insertion of a neural implant in your daughter's brain."

Alba looked alarmed at her parents. *My brain? Why is he talking about my brain? I don't like this.*

"I'll take you through each step now."

The surgeon began drawing on a whiteboard. He drew a leg with a black marker and then added a small box below the knee with tiny cables coming out of it and continued talking.

"The high-tech prosthesis is joined to Alba's bones, muscles, and nerves through a magnetic device inserted in her left leg. This one here," he said, drawing a circle around the box with the blue marker. "The electric device is connected to the leg with electrodes. These here," he said, pointing at the wires coming out of the box. Following that, he sketched the rest of a body using the black marker and included a smaller box inside the head. "A neural sensor will be placed in your daughter's brain," he said redrawing it.

He's not very good in drawing. I'm also not very good.

Alba saw her mom's frowning. Immediately, the neurosurgeon added, "Don't worry; the sensor will be introduced into the brain with a non-invasive procedure through the jugular vein."

Mom has her 'I don't like this' face.

"Please allow me to finish. We will have plenty of time for questions afterwards," the doctor said with a calming gesture, holding out both hands, still full of colored markers.

I want to draw on the board also.

"The neural sensor has microelectrode arrays that deliver and receive signals," he said, drawing another blue circle in the head's box. "The microelectrodes in the brain and in the leg are connected," he added, drawing red lines between them. "They are connected through brain-computer interface technology," he said, writing the letters "BCI." Then, pointing out each word with the marker, he said loudly: "B brain, C computer, I interface, BCI."

BCI, Alba read.

Then, the surgeon drew lines between the head and the knee with the red marker. Her parents followed the drawings attentively.

"Thanks to this technology, the brain and the leg will communicate with each other," he said.

Alba yawned looking around in the room and saw her mom frowning again.

"Don't worry, the communication between the brain and the leg is very smooth. Your daughter will have full mental control over the bionic limb," he said putting the markers down and moving to the corner of the office.

Alba watched the doctor preparing tea in a white porcelain teapot with red flowers on it. He approached with a jar of jam thumbprint cookies. "Please try these, they are delicious."

Alba took one biscuit and, as the surgeon was still holding the jar in front of her, she took another. She ate the biscuits while she watched the surgeon drinking his tea and eating one also. Her parents didn't eat any.

"Allow me to explain to you how Alba will have mental control over the bionic leg," he said.

"Her intention to move the leg will generate activity in the neurons, just as the intention to drink water or listen to music, does. The neural sensor inserted in her brain will pick up the neuronal activity and then will send a message to the electric device in the bionic limb. Then, the bionic leg will move."

Alba yawned again. *This is so boring. How much longer?*

The surgeon continued. "The communication between the brain and the artificial limb will happen in real time, and it'll happen both ways," he added, drawing two arrows with a yellow marker, one from the head to the leg and the other from the leg to the head. "The brain will send information to the bionic leg, and the bionic leg will send information to the brain. The information sent by the bionic limb will trick Alba into believing that the high-tech prosthesis is an actual part of her body," he said with a big smile.

'Trick Alba' he said? Alba looked at her parents who were both frowning now. She was alert. *What?*

"How is this possible you might be thinking? Allow me to explain how. The bionic limb is equipped with sensors that measure different things. For example, ambient temperature. If the temperature was two degrees Celsius, the sensors would send a message to the brain saying, 'it is cold'. The sensors also monitor the pressure on the bionic leg. If we would place a three kilograms box on top of it, the message would be, 'something is heavy'. When the sensors send information, electric signals are formed, and these stimulate areas of the brain. The stimulation triggers the feeling of being cold, of touch, or even pain in the bionic leg. While these sensations are fake, they will feel real to your daughter."

"Mom, how much longer?" Alba asked.

"You need to be patient, sweetheart. We're almost done here," her mom answered.

The surgeon continued talking. "With the brain-computer interface, your daughter will embody a piece of technology as a natural body part. She'll move it as she moves her other leg, feeling no difference. She'll be able to run, walk backwards, step over obstacles, climb stairs, and sit cross-legged. Questions?" he asked.

Alba heard both her parents speaking at the same time asking a million questions about the surgical procedure, the communication between the leg and the brain, and the fake sensations. The doctor listened attentively to all of them, nodded, and took notes in his recycled paper notebook. Then he stood up, grabbed the colored markers from the table again, approached the transparent board, and responded to each question calmly.

Oh, no! he's drawing again. This is going to take forever.

*

Porto, two months after the amputation.

On the way to the OR for her second surgery, Alba panicked: "Nooooo, nooooo, nooooo, I don't want to!"

"Sweetheart, remember what Dr. Angela, told you to do – imagine that you are running with your new leg without any pain."

"Noooo, nooooo, please, Mom, please, noooo!"

"Come on, you can do this. We talked about it. You need to be brave now," her father said.

"Noooooo, nooooo, M tell them I can't!"

"Sweetheart, do what Dr. Angela said, close your eyes and imagine..."

Closing her eyes, she tried to calm down, but she could only picture the ugly white lighting of the intensive care unit. Then, as she remembered the smell of disinfectant and the bedsheets that felt like plastic, she shouted again. "Noooooo! Will my leg be the same as before? Will it? Will it? Will it hurt Mommy? Will it? Will it hurt? Do I have to go? I do not want to go, Mommy, Mommy, Mommmmmmmmy pleeeeease!"

She continued shouting until the anesthesia spread through her body, rendering her unconscious.

*

Porto, three and a half months after the amputation.

"Ms. you can do it – we have a deal. Four steps equal a half chocolate muffin; eight steps equal a whole one," Ramon told her.

"I can't. I'm going to fall. I can't. M, you tell Ramon I can't."

"You certainly can. You already lifted your new leg nicely twice. Now, you're going to take a few steps with this. You will because you can. Only a few. Don't worry, you won't fall."

Alba looked at Ramon, frowning. He stood in front of her holding a walker with both hands. Ramon was always nice and gentle. And his muffins were yummy. She looked down at her bionic leg, then back to Ramon and then around, in the gym. *Where is the chocolate muffin?*

"Four steps – one muffin?"

"No, I said four steps equal half chocolate muffin and eight steps equal a whole one."

Alba stared at the large muscles in his arms, then at his thick, dark hair styled with gel, and shook her head.

"How do you know I won't fall?"

"Alba, go now. You put your hands on the walker and go."

She shook her head again.

"Come on, we talked about it – it's part of our plan to get you back into football, remember?"

"I don't want to fall."

"What if M is by your side?" Ramon asked.

"Okay, M can hold the walker. M is very strong. You too, Ramon, but M is machine-strong."

"Yes, M can hold, by my side."

With M and Ramon holding the walker, she took her first steps with the bionic leg, and she got the chocolate muffin.

Enjoying it seated on a mattress on the floor, she asked, "M, where were you yesterday? Where did you go?"

"I went to the operations branch."

"What for?"

"Maintenance."

"Are you hurt?"

"No."

"Why are you wearing a black bandage below your knee then? Do you want to look like rapper? Ana Luisa said once that she saw a DJ at a party and that there was a rapper also, but I didn't believe her, I think she saw a video, but she said it was a party."

"I am not hurt. I am not wearing a black bandage. I am wearing an elastic compressed band."

"You're funny. That's a bandage. And nobody wears a bandage unless they are hurt. I've got a bandage, look, big one, look. But I didn't get a black one, they put me only white bandages in this hospital. I don't like it with my new leg, can we go home now?"

*

Porto, four months after the amputation.

"Mommy, can I have more orange juice, please? And can I have a chocolate croissant? I don't like this plain croissant very much. When do we go home?" she asked for the third time nibbling the pastry.

Alba was in a very good mood because it was her last day in hospital. Looking under the bedsheets at the bionic leg, her face lit up. *I look like M.*

Because it was her last day, the hospital personnel had added a croissant and chocolate custard to her dinner tray. Eating the first spoon of the custard, she believed she was in the best hospital in the world and decided to ask for more when an orderly picked up the tray later. Cheerful after eating the croissant, she called to M from the bed, "M, M, listen, listen. Can you imagine if you only had three hairs like this?" she asked, with three fingers pointing up on top of her head. "You'd look like a pineapple, M. Would you like that, M? Would you? No? No? Why? Why wouldn't you like it?" she asked and then burst into laughter.

M listened to her, and then, silently, put the soft pink blanket over her.

"I'm not cold, M."

"The room temperature will continue dropping fast at this time."

"Thank you," she said with a smile. As she opened a comic book and changed position, the blanket fell off the bed.

"Oops," she said looking at it and then at M.

"I increased the room temperature by two degrees," M said picking up the blanket.

"No, you didn't, you haven't moved."

"I connected via Bluetooth with the smart temperature sensor."

"The what what?" Alba asked rolling her eyes. "Never mind, I'm busy here," she said theatrically and then turned her attention back to the comic book.

After reading a few pages, she called her mom: "Mommy, Mommy, Mommy! Look, look, look, look here. The cat ate the cake," she said pointing at the colorful pages.

Her mom approached the bed and caressed her hair lovingly.

Taking her hands, she said very seriously, "Mom, I've got two very important questions. Do you think that there is a swimming pool in this hospital? And can I have potato chips?"

"No, I don't think there is a swimming pool in this hospital. And no, no potato chips today," her mom answered laughing. "Now I will leave you with M for a short while sweetheart, I'll have a quick dinner at the cafeteria, make some calls and come back, all right? You can watch cartoons."

Alba had switched on the screen before her mother finished the sentence.

After a while, she turned her attention to M, "M, I want a black cat. Can we have a black cat? Can you ask

Mommy and Daddy? I like black cats, you know? They are like dogs. they think they are dogs. I also like dogs," she said looking at the screen. Turning to M, she continued, "I know how to train a dog, I know; do you know? I can teach you if you want. If you want the dog to catch like a stick or something, you do this many times," she said, moving her right arm up and down. "You do like this; you see, like this. Then you throw the stick. Are you listening, M? What did I say? So, we need to get a bed for the dog and a leash to go to the beach. Did you like the brown dog on the beach the other day? I think it was a Labrador. Was it? I am not sure if Labradors are so big. But I like it. Ahhh, I am tired." She yawned, grabbed M's arm, and laid down.

As she continued watching cartoons quietly, she heard a knock on the door. Without waiting to be invited in, a tall man wearing a white doctor's coat entered the room. She didn't recognize him, but, as medical personnel came into the room constantly, she didn't find it strange. She looked at him. He stood in front of the bed for a while without saying anything. Finally, he spoke. "Good evening, how are you feeling?"

Alba felt a chill in her spine.

"I'm good thank you," she said and then continued watching cartoons ignoring him.

What does he want?

"I understand that you are fully recovered now..."

"Why are you bald? Were you born without hair, or did it fall out later? Will I be bald also? Daddy says I shouldn't eat a lot of chocolate. Can I get bald if I eat a lot of chocolate?" Then, looking at M she said, "I want my mommy. M, call my mommy."

"I'm glad to see that you are fully recovered. Good night to you," he said and left.

Alba remained silent for a while.

"M, who was that?" she asked almost whispering. "I didn't like him. First, I thought it was someone bringing potato chips because I asked mom before if I could have some, and then it was a doctor. And I didn't like him. He was very pale and had almost no eyebrows. Who was the tall doctor, M?"

"Dr. Östmann."

"Who is Dr. Östmann?"

"Dr. Östmann is the chief data scientist at the Hölfang Foundation and the director of the eMotional-Machine program. He is my creator."

"And why did he come here? Is he my new doctor now? I had a chill, here," she said touching a space on her lower back. That doctor is not good for me, M, I know. I can tell when someone is not good for me. I told you about it. I don't know why, but I know. Is he going to hurt me? Call my mommy please. I want my mommy. I want to go home. I don't like here," she said, crying softly.

HELICONIUS BUTERFLIES

Porto, May 29, 2013.

"Double espresso, no milk, please." Dr. Östmann told the waiter at the Foundation cafeteria.

"Dr. Östmann! Good morning!" A voice said from behind him.

"Dr. Garcia, good morning. How are you today?" he said, turning around.

"Good, good, I'm glad I found you here. I didn't see you yesterday."

"How is your research with rats going Dr. Garcia?"

"As a matter of fact..."

Oh, no, here he goes... Every time he says 'as a matter of fact' it is a long story.

"The experiment with mice is proving to be very successful. Last week we tested the latest BCI developed by the Engineering Unit and the results were good. I'm confident that the experiment will shed new light on the treatment of mental depression. Depression is becoming the disease of the century, Dr. Östmann, the disease of the century. It's not only common in adults nowadays but it's been increasing during the last decade among teenagers, and, according to the latest figures, it is on the rise in adolescence. It's just a matter of time to see an increase on child depression. Are you tired?"

"Excuse me?"

"You look tired, did you have trouble sleeping last night?"

Dr. Östmann looked down at the corpulent head of the Applied-Psychology unit and his extra-large mustache.

Remember, he's been working at the Foundation for five years and you just arrived. He's a good source of information about internal procedures and about 'who is who'.

"Yes, I'm a bit tired," he answered putting his hand on his belly.

"Upset stomach also? Is it a special day today?"

"It's not but I'll brief the Foundation's board on progress on the eMotional-Machine program this morning."

"Are things going well with the program."

"Oh, yes, yes, indeed."

"It's a personal matter then."

"What is?"

"The cause of your difficulty sleeping last night and having an upset stomach this morning."

"I don't know."

"Is it a special date for you perhaps today?"

Dr. Östmann made an effort to continue the conversation, thinking again that it was in his interest to be friendly with Dr. Garcia.

"Well, today was my wedding anniversary. But I'm divorced, as you know."

"Dr. Östmann, if I may, I recently read a study that explained that people who resent their ex-partners develop health issues. As a matter of fact, resentment was commonly described as 'acid going from the stomach to the mouth'."

"That's very interesting, I appreciate your concern. Did you hear anything new about the Foundation's confidentiality policy?" he asked, changing the topic, somewhat annoyed with Dr Garcia.

"Only that there are no plans to change it."

"But how can the Foundation's board be so afraid of criticism?"

"I wouldn't say it's the Foundation's board, I'd say it's the CEO of Hölfang Industries, he's the one who makes all the important decisions."

"Yes, but because of the clause, the world doesn't know about our work. It's absurd that the world doesn't know about the work that excellent scientists such as yourself do."

"I agree with you, I do."

"HR did a good job tricking me into this situation when I accepted the job. But I addressed the board on this point already and I'll do it again."

Looking at his watch, he finished his double espresso with a long sip, put the cup down, and left, saying, "Nice talk. Good morning to you."

Leaving the cafeteria, his stomach reacted to the double espresso. He would never accept it but maybe Dr. Garcia was right. Last night, he tossed around in his white-and-yellow striped pyjamas in bed for hours. His wedding anniversary brought bad memories back. He had met his ex-wife, Mairead, when he was studying for a master's degree in Ireland. It was love at first sight, and they got married without knowing each other. Four years later, she had cheated on him with a colleague and left him. 'He's sweeter to me than you are' she had said to him as explanation. Since then, he didn't smile much. This morning, he woke up with an upset stomach and the words 'he's sweeter to me than you are' replaying in his mind.

Feeling a bitter taste in his mouth, he stopped walking, put his right hand on his chin, and reflected about his sleepless night. *Last night, I felt the need to shout that my ex-wife had been unfair to me, but there was nobody listening. Then, I slept after taking a sleeping pill and I had a nightmare in which my skin cracked. And now Dr. Garcia. It's all nonsense. I'm sure the study he mentioned lacks scientific proof. My stomach is upset because of the Indian food takeaway I had yesterday for dinner. Too spicy.* He took an antacid tablet and continued walking.

He strode down the marble hallway in the north wing of the Hölfang Foundation on his way to the main conference room to brief the board on the progress under the eM-M program. Looking down, he noticed the black and white checkered flooring. *I never noticed this flooring before... it looks like a chessboard.*

*

Dr. Östmann arrived at the conference room a few minutes ahead of the meeting. In front of the large mahogany door, he tucked his stripped grey cotton shirt into his brown chinos. *My ex-wife used to tell me that I shouldn't wear grey because the color enhances the paleness of my skin.* He removed the bitter thought by running his fingers through his hair, checked the time again, and at 8:00 a.m. sharp, he entered.

He looked at the board members who were seated at a luxurious titanium conference table. "Good morning, gentlemen," he said and then went around the table, greeting each of them.

"Mr. Chen, good to see you fully recovered, sir."

"Mr. Austin, did you enjoy the skiing holiday with your family?"

"Mr. Kendrick, nice watch!"

"Mr. Sengupta, very pleased to meet you sir."

"Mr. Odongo, how are your children?"

"Mr. Ramirez, we need to plan for that dinner."

"Mr. Beckhoff, always good to see you."

"Dr. Esteves, I look forward to your feedback today."

Then he sat at the end of the conference table. *Good that I only have to do this occasionally.*

When the chairman arrived a few minutes later, he began the briefing. "Good morning again, gentlemen. I'm pleased to inform you that Phase I of eMotional-Machine program (the eM-M-p), called Symbiosis 1.0 was completed successfully. Today, I'll brief you on what I have achieved. But before that, as today is Mr. Sengupta first board meeting, I will explain the big picture first."

He stood up and walked around the table talking: "The term symbiosis comes from the Greek 'symbiōsis' and means 'state of living together'. In this state, one species can benefit from another at the host's expense. This is the case for roundworms and dogs for example. In other cases, one of the species benefits from the other without harming it. Such as orchids growing in trees. In other cases, the relationship is mutually beneficial, as with coral and algae."

The board room was quiet, and his voice was the only sound.

"Humans and machine workers live in symbiosis. They are as coral and algae, their relationship is mutually beneficial. I intent to prove with the eM-M-p that if humans and machine workers become more alike, the benefits of living together will increase, for both. This is my thesis."

Dr. Östmann served himself a coffee, enjoying that the board members waited for him to continue. After sipping it, he continued talking from the end of the table. "Now to the achievements of Phase I. With Symbiosis 1.0, machine_M and subject_A are more alike," he paused. "Yes, you heard me correctly. More alike," he said pressing a button on a control panel embedded in the conference table.

The lights in the conference room dimmed and large holograms of Alba and M appeared in behind him.

"With symbiosis 1.0, machine_M and subject_A are more alike," he repeated. "A fragment of machine_M was embedded in subject_A and a fragment of subject_A was embedded in machine_M." He made the holograms juxtaposed behind him.

"Following the amputation of her left leg," he continued, "subject_A had a bionic prosthesis attached. The prosthesis was developed by the Engineering unit and includes a piece that was taken from machine_M. Machine_M is connected to the piece through a micro-Bluetooth and it 'believes' that its part of its own system."

He sipped his coffee before continuing: "Why did I do this? I did it to trick machine_M into believing a part of itself 'lives' in subject_A. Why? As per the Foundation's protocols, all AI prototypes are designed to be responsible to monitor that their systems up to date. This happens with the support of the Maintenance unit, of course. I expect that making Machine_M believe that a piece of its systems lives in subject_A will create a bond with subject_A."

He paused, looked at the holograms and then continued: "At the same time, living tissue extracted from subject_A during the leg amputation was embedded into machine_M." Noticing that some board members reacted, he explained it further: "This is very experimental, because, as you know, success of human living tissue growing outside a laboratory environment is challenging. Machine_M has been programmed to know that the human tissue belongs to subject_A and that it is its duty to protect it," he said. "Ideally, the human living tissue would grow and expand over machine_M but this is again, highly experimental. Also, ideally subject_A will need more machine components in the near future," he said as the holograms vanished.

He pressed another button on the command panel. "Symbiosis 1.0 concluded successfully yesterday. You will see images of the procedures now," he said. Video images filled the white walls, ceiling, and flooring of the conference room. Some board members looked skeptical, but most were curious, and some were impressed. When the video ended, the room was quiet. Then, the chairman stood up and clapped softly. One by one first and then at a time, the rest joined him. The soft clapping grew louder, and the room was filled with praise for Dr. Östmann.

"Thank you, gentlemen, thank you. There is no need, really," he said breathing in the praise. "Please, please, allow me to continue."

He moved to a side of the room. "So, machine_M and subject_A look more alike now. But what about their behavior?" He paused as if waiting for an answer and then continued: "How do species become more similar in nature? The answer is through mimicry. Mimicry is a natural mechanism by which some species learn to resemble the behavioral patterns of others. It is used by the Heliconius butterfly, for example, to defend itself against predators. The butterfly mimics the colors and patterns of other species that are toxic for birds," he said, projecting a hologram of the insect on top of the conference table.

"Machines already mimic human motion and human behavior but what about emotions? As you know, machine_M is learning to mimic emotions from subject_A. Let me tell you about the achievements during Phase I." Dr. Östmann approached the table and drank some water.

"You all know well that machines used to learn with traditional methods that limited the types of knowledge and skills that they could gain. These old techniques relied on large volumes of training data from different sources. With my method, inspired by the principle of mimicry, machine_M learns from a single source: subject_A. Many doubted about this approach, but you understood my rationale and had the vision to support me because you are all visionaries," he said, smiling.

"Your judgement was good, gentlemen. The collection of training data is ongoing successfully and today I announce that I expect machine_M to write the first algorithm to reproduce a human emotion very soon."

On this point, the board clapped and praised him again. "Gentlemen, please, allow me to continue..."

*

About an hour later, the scientist headed back to his office down the black-and-white marble hallway again. *Next time, I'll address the issue of the confidentially policy. The world should know about Symbiosis 1.0. It deserves to know. The board members lack the courage that is needed to achieve something grand.* He continued walking.

Well... As they like secrets, I have a secret of my own. Dr. Garcia's experiment with rats inspired me. If the girl gets depressed, her emotions will be biased, and M won't learn pure human emotions. To think that I almost overlooked this... But I've addressed it now, the special feature I included in the BCI is sending electrical currents towards the girl's pineal gland. Just like with Dr Garcia's rats, the serotonin levels in her brain will remain stable and prevent depression. I need to manage all the risks this time. I can't fail again, or I will become just another scientist with a great idea that I have failed to implement. I won't let people think I have failed again, like they believed with my last job. I could tell the little girl was scared when she saw me, but she will be the perfect subject. THE BCI WILL DO THAT.

As he walked, he had pain in his stomach and a bitter taste in the mouth again. Back to his office, he gave instructions to his assistant that he was not to be bothered with calls or colleagues for the rest of the day.

BACK

Porto, June 01, 2013.

Walking home from the bus stop after her first day back to school, Alba realized that despite having played football and tag at school, she didn't have any pain in the leg. *I have no pain! I like my new leg now.*

"M, you know why I love having new shoes?" she asked. "You know why? It is because I see them a lot. Of course, M! It's because I look at my feet a lot when I have new shoes, and then I see them, and I like them very much. I like looking at my new shoes; my mom brought them for me yesterday because I needed new shoes because I've got a new leg." *I love my mommy.*

"Mommy, Mommy," she called when she got home. "I played football and tag today. I didn't score any goals, but Julia did, and I played, and we won. Beatriz said something nasty about my new leg, and Matilda also, but

I didn't care because M was with me, and I didn't care. She is not nice, Matilda. Can I watch cartoons?"

"I'm glad you had a good first day back at school sweetheart. And, no, you can't watch cartoons today. Today is not Wednesday. Wednesday is Cartoon Day."

Alba ran to her bedroom and came back with a ball. "Mommy, I want to play with all my toys. You didn't bring me this green ball to the hospital. I like this one. Mommy, can I sleep in the living today? Tomorrow, I'm going to play football at school. I don't like Beatriz, but she doesn't play football. I like Leonela, she's my friend. Beatriz, I don't like her because she's not nice. Can I sleep in the living room today? Can I sleep on the sofa and watch movies?"

Without waiting for an answer, she ran around the house looking for more toys. "Look M, look, my tiger!" she said, grabbing a large stuffed animal that was under the sofa.

She continued running, playing, and laughing around the house, with M following her in silence.

Later in the evening, too excited to go to sleep, she sat at the kitchen counter in her pyjamas.

"M, you know what? I know how to make pancakes. Do you want to see? I can do pancakes by myself. We need flour, eggs, and... I do not remember what else. Mommy knows. Can you ask Mommy? Do you like pancakes? Can I make pancakes? Can I have pancakes with..." When her mom entered the kitchen and signaled the time to her, she realized she was in trouble, so she sprinted upstairs to her room.

On the way, she was moody. She wanted pancakes, but her mom only allowed her to have them on Saturday mornings. *I love my mommy, but I don't like that cartoon day is only Wednesday and pancake is only Saturday, I love pancakes.* "MMMMM, is it Saturday tomorrow? Can I have pancakes tomorrow? MMMMM!"

In bed, she crashed, exhausted from the excitement and the physical exercise of her first day back to school.

*

Before she walked into the land of dreams, she heard a familiar song in the distance. 'Waves, waves, waves of blue…' The music lured her to the ocean. There, waves rocked and enveloped her in a powerful but tender roar.

Looking around she realized that she was standing on a large rock close to a beach. She was calm. She recognized the place; she had been there before. Water surrounded her. *It is nice to be so close to the water.*

Then, she stood at the beach, bare feet on the sand, still listening to the song and the waves.

And she sensed Her. Warm and immense, like the sun, like the ocean.

After a while, she saw Her, facing the waves from the shore.

She was surrounded by a white and golden light, that radiated from within and shimmered around Her. In

Her presence, Alba felt like floating, as if everything moved in slow motion around Her. As if there were no time or space. As if time and space had a different meaning in Her presence. Looking at Her, she felt an immense love, a love from beyond this world and her eyes filled up with tears.

She knew that she had been close to Her many nights, and always, saw Her from a distance. But something felt different tonight.

Alba continued looking at Her while She still faced the ocean. She noted Her long hair, her robe, and a delicate golden net draped over it fluttering in the breeze. Turning, She said without words, "You have come. You found me."

"Oh, I love you so much, so, so much. I have missed you so much. I miss being with you all the time. I miss you always," Alba said also without words.

Then she felt blue, as She was, as water. She felt Her waves around, a bubble of light, and Her voice in the distance but close at the same time: "As the mother takes care of her children, as the general takes care of her soldiers, as the queen fairy takes care of the little ones, I always care of you... I always accompany you... I have always been by your side and will always be... Because I vowed to take care of you before time... Do not forget Alba. Do not forget me. Come and find me again."

Hearing these words, Alba had a moment of awareness. She knew she had to remember Her and Her message. She knew that she needed to find Her again and that she had to remember Her. She had to as if her life depended on it.

CRASHED

Porto, June 07, 2013.

Dr. Östmann was absorbed by work in his office designing a new feature for the AI prototypes under the eM-M-p. It was late but he didn't mind, no one was waiting for him at home. He tried not to think whether his commitment to his work had meant he faded from the lives of his friends and family save for the occasional birthday or Christmas party, or whether his lack of connection had driven him to his work. Whatever it was, working late nights and weekends was now part of his routine. The only thing that bothered him about staying late in the office was that the cafeteria was closed, so if he was hungry, he had to order takeaway and he didn't like waiting for the order.

He bent over his graphite-toned metal desk, which was isolated in the middle of his office, like an island. He worked on the 'tear device'. Dropping his pencil, he looked at his notes. *The logic is quite simple: after a combination of pre-defined keywords are spoken, the eye drop container activates and releases fake tears. After, 'I got really hurt', three tears will be released in each eye. After, 'I'm sorry for your loss,' ten tears.* Satisfied, Dr. Östmann read the list of tasks to do. 1- Train the tear device to recognized Machine_M voice; 2- Define categories for the causes of crying (grief, loss, and pain to be included); 3 - Define the combination of keywords for each category; 4 - Test the texture of different liquids for the tears and 5- Develop a system to monitor the volume of tears in each container to refill automatically.

Ouch, my back. It hasn't been the same since the injury on that hunting trip. He stood up to stretch, then looked up at the wall-mounted roe deer's head that decorated one of his office walls and, as if inspired by it, added some numbers to his notebook. Then, he approached the glass wall on his left side and looked inside at prototypes 01 to 08 of the eM-M-p. They all looked like M because there were earlier versions of it. He would test the tear device on one or two of them before incorporating it into M, prototype 09.

His mind went back to task number 2: Define categories for the causes of crying (grief, loss, and pain to be included). *So, when will you cry M? What will make you cry? What will be the thresholds for each category? You'll be so likable when you cry. You'll win people over easily because people are programmed to believe that there is good in those who cry. Mairead, cried all the time. If I would speak too harshly, she cried. If I was busy with my work and didn't have time for her, she cried. Crying, crying, crying, always. Because she cried, I thought she was good, and then she cheated on me.*

Thinking about his ex-wife upset him, so he moved to the opposite side of his office, and, through the glass wall, he looked at the server room of the eM-M-p. Staring at the cables, racks, switches, and lights and listening to the computer humming, he calmed down.

He then stared at the nine large monitors wall mounted behind his desk. They livestreamed the activity of each of the nine prototypes. Before sitting back on his desk, he used a control panel to dim the stainless-steel recessed ceiling lighting in the office and increased the light on the reading lamp. Then, he focused on formulating an index to calculate the number of tears for the categories 'grief, loss and pain'.

*

A soft, repetitive beep distracted him. First, he ignored it. As it continued, he turned, lowered his reading glasses, and checked the monitors on his back to identify the source of the beep. "M," he said out loud, standing up and approaching monitor 09.

He examined the array of windows and data on display and immediately understood their meaning. Deciphering the algorithms on the screen, he felt victorious. *There it is.*

"I did it! I did it! I did it!" he exclaimed loudly, raising his arms in the air. Approaching the black leather rolling chair close to the monitor, he studied the algorithms. After a few minutes, he stood up and announced to an invisible audience: "Ladies and gentlemen, I present you the formula for joy."

Afterwards, he studied the notes added by M on the formula, reading them aloud to himself.

"Trigger. Joy is triggered in subject_A by an external stimulus. The catalyst is something anticipated, such as receiving a gift on her birthday, or unanticipated, such as finding an insect in the bathroom ceiling at school. Environmental factors (including atmospheric pressure, temperature, wind speed, humidity, and sunlight) do not influence how the stimulus is perceived outdoors. Indoor conditions (including size of the room or light) do not influence this either."

"Effect. Subject_A experiences a combination of surprise, delight, and gladness in response to the stimulus. There is a non-linear correlation between the size or the uniqueness of the incentive and the response to it. A large or a small portion of chocolate cake have the same effect, but an exotic spider provokes a stronger reaction than a common one."

"Facial expression. The most distinctive element is a prolonged smile, that lasts over ten seconds. With the smile, the corners of subject_A's lips are drawn, the muscles around the eyes are tightened, the forehead softens, the eyebrows are lifted, and crow's feet appear.

"Body. Expressing joy, subject_A gestures more than the average person. She often claps and takes short jumps while talking. The heart and breathing rates increase (in linear proportion to the size of the smile and body movement)."

"Speech characteristics. The speech rate, volume, and pitch, rise in line with the intensity of the emotion and are higher than average. 'Ahh' (delight), 'oh' (surprise), 'I'm so lucky!' (good fortune), 'yes!' (success), 'wow!' (admiration), and 'I like this' (content) are the verbal expressions used more frequently. A range of uncategorized melodic phrases such as 'la, la, la' or 'tan, tan, ta ran' are also used."

*

"I did it, I did it, I did it," Dr. Östmann repeated again after reading the notes. He considered ordering a bottle of champagne to celebrate his triumph for a brief moment, but instead decided to continue working with a clear head. Content, he went back to calculating thresholds.

After a while, a beeping noise interrupted his calculations once again. This time, it wasn't the same soft, repetitive beep from before; it was a loud alarm that infiltrated his office.

He jumped out of the chair and scrutinized the monitors.

"M?" he asked with his gaze fixed on one of the computer screens.

"M? M?" he asked reaching for a keyboard.

Before he could type anything, the monitor went off.

The data scientist was startled. *There is only one possible explanation why the monitor is off. It's off because M switched off, but M is not programmed to switch off. How did it happen?*

He continued looking at the blank screen and pressing control keys on the keyboard as if hoping to revive the machine by doing that.

"No, no, no, no!" he growled.

M is off and I can't reboot its systems. This isn't supposed to happen.

He ran his fingers through his hair a few times, staring at the server room. *I need to stay calm. There is only one thing to do now. He pressed a yellow button on the control panel on his desk. The removal protocol is launched, M will be back here tonight. It'll be dissected, and I'll find out what happened.*

The scientist stroked his hair several times again. Then, he tucked his shirt into his trousers and continued working. *I'll fix this. It won't look like I failure. I won't be seen as a failure, not again.*

GONE

Porto. June 08, 2013.

Alba was glad to see both her parents waiting for her at the bus stop back from school.

"Mommy, Daddy!" she said hugging them. "You know? before I was in the hospital, I wrote my name in Greek letters at school. I forgot about it. I found this in my backpack. Let me show you," she said dropping her backpack on the street and taking out a wrinkled piece of paper. "You see?" She showed them the paper. "I did it at school. I know it is Greek because my teacher, Ms. Sophia is Greek, and these are Greek letters. You see? This is my name, with Greek letters. This is the A, this is the L, this is the B, and this is the A in Greek letters. I wrote my name in Greek," she repeated putting the paper down and staring at them.

"So?" she asked rolling a little ball of blue tac in her hands awaiting a reaction.

"Oh, right. You wrote your name in Greek, very good job sweetheart, wonderful," her mom said taking her school back and holding her hand.

"Very nice," her father added.

Alba smiled. *My mommy is so beautiful. I love my mommy. I like her blue jumpsuit; she looks very elegant. I love my daddy also.*

Entering home, Alba called her friend: "MMMMM! MMMMM! MMMMM! Where are you? I have news from school, come here yooooouuuuuu!"

As M didn't answer, Alba joined her parents to the living room.

"You know? The man did this many times," she said standing in front of them and moving an arm up and down. "But he did not feel anything. You know what he did? You know what he did?"

Her parents looked at her.

"Who?" her father asked.

"I mean the gentleman. He, the gentleman, took the needle and put it inside the ball. You know that needles have a ball at the end?" she paused. As she got no answer, she continued: "A ball at the end, yes, a ball at the end. Then, the gentleman took the needle and put it in until the ball, in the real hand of the gentleman, and then he didn't feel anything. And you know what he did? Then he took the paper and he put it inside the ball. Do you know that there is a needle in the arm?"

Her parents looked at each other, looking perplex.

"But do you know that there is a needle in the arm?" she asked.

"Where did you see all that, sweetheart?" her dad asked.

"On TV! It's magic. He's a gentleman who has done magic since he was little."

"Ahhh, so you are telling us about a magic trick that you saw on TV," her mom said.

"Yes!" she said, pleased that her parents understood.

"Very nice," her dad said.

"M, where are you?" she asked again and running upstairs looking for her companion. "Where are you? Time to play," she said going to the kitchen now. She took four oat and chocolate chip biscuits from the pantry and waited to hear the familiar sound of M walking. As she waited and heard nothing, she felt a knot forming in her throat. Walking slowly and quiet, as if making a noise was going to make the situation worse, she went back to the living room where her parents were still seated.

"Mom, Dad, where is M?" she asked almost whispering. "And Dad, why are you home so early?"

"I'm so sorry, teddy bear, we have something to tell you."

"Mom, what is happening?" Alba asked.

"Sweetheart, M is not here."

"But this morning you said..."

"I know sweetheart, I told you that M went to the Maintenance unit at the Foundation, and it'd be back this evening."

"When is M coming back?" she asked pressing the biscuits in her hand.

"That's what we need to talk to you about," her dad said.

"Listen…"

But Alba didn't. As her parents talked, she just kept on pressing the cookies in her hand harder and harder. She didn't want to listen to them, she just wanted to see M, like every day.

"… I'm so sorry… M isn't coming back… We're so sorry… Some people came last night and took M… We thought it would be better to tell you… We don't know what happened… You can't visit M because it's not allowed… You can't say goodbye…"

M isn't coming back. M isn't coming back.

She touched her left leg. But *I need M. I need M by my side. They lied to me. Mom said it would be back this evening. Why did they lie to me? Why didn't they keep M here with me? Why did M leave?*

"Sweetheart? Are you listening to what we are saying?"

But she wasn't, she didn't want to, she just wanted M back.

"You said it was coming back! Why did you lie to me? Why? Where is M? Why isn't it here? Did you tell it to go? I want M to be here, and I need to climb a rope in school at the gym and it's very high and I don't know if I can. And I like talking to M. I tell M many things you don't understand! I want M to be here with me!"

"But sweetheart, there's nothing we—" her mom said.

Unable to bare the news, she opened her hand, dropping the cookie crumbs on the floor and rushed to her room slamming the door.

EXOSKELETONS AND FRANCESINHAS

Porto, February 01, 2033.

Alba checked the time. Isongo had told her that the research team of the Instituto de Pensamento would be meeting in the area in front of the former central altar in ten minutes for a brainstorming session. She looked at the shiny Baroque gilding and the polychromate wood carvings as she waited. Some colleagues arrived and sat on different sections of a massive brown curved modular sofa. Alba counted her colleagues as they arrived, she had met so many people this morning that she didn't remember how many of them were in the research team. Then she thought about the briefing with Ms. Vivian. She had told Alba that the Foundation had eight-hundred-and ten-employees and that twenty percent of them were machine workers, which meant a hundred and sixty-two. She wondered what she could do to find out about M as her access to the Foundation programs and operations were limited to her job as junior researcher.

Then, she reflected about how much she had gained from participating in the eM-M-p.

With the education grant, I went to an international school, and I learnt English. Later, I was able to study abroad at top class universities. And now I have this great job opportunity. A job at a thinktank and in Porto, it couldn't be better. Dad says I'm a 'natural thinker' and that 'I'm always keen to learn new ways to interpret things', I guess that's why a job at a 'thinking institute' is so appealing to me.

She sat and smiled at her colleagues as they continued gathering.

I guess I've been lucky in my life. I grew up in a beautiful place pampered by parents, who cherish me and do the best for me every day. True that as adolescent and as I teen I got quite frustrated with them, but I think that's normal. I guess Mom and Dad can't complain, I was always a disciplined student and I'm now a 'solid' professional as my former boss used to say.

She checked the time again.

*

As soon as the director, Dr. Badeaux, arrived, he started the brainstorming session. "Good morning, everybody. Welcome, welcome. And a special welcome to Dr. Alba, the newest addition to the research team. Today we launch our next research piece. But before we get to that, Dr. Alba, I know you met everybody before with Dr. Isongo, but, please, share your academic background with us."

"Thank you, Dr. Badeaux. Good morning, again everybody. I have a bachelor's degree in philosophy from the London School of Economics and Political Science in the UK, and a Ph.D. at the University of Pittsburgh in the US. My thesis is entitled 'Commonalities of Philosophical Branches in the Modern Era'. After my Ph.D., I worked as assistant professor at the University of Pittsburgh until two months ago, when I left to join you here."

"Thank you, Dr. Alba, I'm very pleased to have you in the team. Now, let's focus on our next research piece – 'Understanding the complexities of transhumanism'. I want us to explore together different angles to analyse the topic. Questions? I'm joking, no questions until I open the floor for a dialogue. I'm joking again, you can ask questions any time."

The director had a strong French accent, so Alba did as other colleagues were doing, and followed a live transcript displayed on screens suspended from the ceiling.

"Transhumanism is trending. And yet, there is no agreement about what it is. A philosophical movement? Scientific? Social? All of them combined perhaps? There is no agreement. Yet, it gains popularity. Day by day. We can see an explosion of conferences, in the last years. Blogs, news articles, and books. Disseminating its ideas and aspirations. What is it transhumanism? in essence? I ask. What does is it to our modern era? I also ask. Those questions, we will address. As a team. That is our work now."

Some colleagues nodded and others made notes on tablets with covers that matched their outfits.

"Now, icebreaker. You say the first thing in your mind. First thing. When you hear 'transhumanism', what do you think? Fast. Don't overthink. Say your first thoughts, one or two sentences, no more. One or two. I will pass the turn to the next person when I switch the light under your seat. Be alert! You don't know who will go next. Just to make it a bit funnier. Adriana, you first. Fast, fast," he said tapping his tablet and making a neon light under her seat switch on.

"Transhumanists believe that the human condition can be upgraded with technology."

As she finished the sentence, Alba saw a word cloud appeared in the screens and the words 'human condition', and 'technology' flashed in green neon.

"I want to be super strong."

"Diseases limit human life, and transhumanism offers a way to protect us against them."

"Some people say that transhumanism is unethical."

"Aging is a disease that technology can overcome."

Alba listened and followed the lights under the seats and the changing word cloud that was updated with each intervention in real time.

"Enhancing the human body with technology is a good thing."

"I don't know what to think."

"The goal of transhumanism is not to turn humans into cyborgs, as some people say."

"Transhumanism is the modern Holy Grail."

"Human life is improved with technological advancement."

"I wish I had super sight."

"Humans are already enhanced with machine components."

Alba was the last one to speak. "I have a bionic leg."

"Very good. Very good," the director said. "Now we will think more. A second round now. Thinking. Deeper into the topic. We do a second round, and you can explain your thought. Don't worry about coherence. We will go with the flow. Thinking. No need to wait for the light. Alba, you were last, you speak first now."

Alba was taken aback for being asked to be the first one to speak but then she thought that she had always spoken openly about her bionic leg and relaxed.

"Technology has improved my life. With it, I overcame a disease and improved my physical condition," she said lifting her dress and showing her bionic limb. "Without it, my health and my physical movement wouldn't be as good as they are. My life is better because of high-tech. I recognize that I am not one-hundred-percent organic because part of my left leg is made of steel instead of flesh, but I don't consider myself a cyborg. I'm enhanced by technology. My bionic leg, is as much a part of me as the rest of my body is."

"Good example," Dr. Badeaux said. "Medical AI advanced fast. Now, many practices heal, improve human capacities. Deep brain stimulation for neurological disorders of motor skills. Parkinson's. Memory implants for Alzheimer's, dementia. Doctors can cure illnesses not curable before. That is thanks to AI."

After the director spoke, colleagues followed.

"I believe that people should reach their higher potential with technology. Having super hearing, super eyesight, and super strength are possible and should be available for all."

"Brain-computer interfaces, sensory modification, neurostimulation, and exoskeletons are super cool and are super ready to help us overcoming diseases and aging. Why should biology determine us? Human augmentation can and should be done integrating machine components in the body."

"Exoskeletons are the best example. Super soldiers are not a fantasy any longer. Enhancements are good, are useful. When I look at them, what I think is: can the perfect human be created? Then, I asked myself: what makes a human, human?"

"To answer that, I'd ask what is humankind in essence? And, what to expect if we alter it?"

"Different theories explain the origin of the planet Earth and human life on it. Regardless of the theory, one could think that humankind and planet Earth originated as a binomial. What this means is that each one is the way it is because of the other. So, what happens if we alter one of them?"

"Are you saying that humankind and Earth are components of a higher system and as that the system's balance is based on the synergies between the components? What happens if the integrity of the components is compromised then? Will the system be then unbalanced?"

"What happens? Maybe something similar to climate change. Human activities (transportation for example) produce emissions of green gases that go into the atmosphere. Pollution affects the integrity of the Earth. Then, because on the increased gases, the Earth goes into 'global warming'. And then, global warming causes rising sea levels that result in human migration."

"So, you're applying the Systems Theory framework, right? The theory that says that a change in a component of a system affects the overall system."

"Yes, with transhumanism and the embedment of mechatronic parts into the human body, the integrity of the human body is affected. The human body is made of organic matter, so changing that nature might have an effect on the overall system. What will be the consequences of this?"

Alba followed the discussion taking notes on her tablet.

"The consequences? The consequences are that humans can be perfected. Why live with disease? Why live with weaknesses?"

"There is no need. AI can perfect humans. I don't want to suffer illnesses that reduce my potential. I don't want to accept weakness in my life, in my body, or in my mind. Disease and fragility serve me for nothing. I say no to them."

"Yes, why aging? Aging is the worst epidemic affecting humankind. As we age, we turn weak and dependent. We lose potential and need to relay on others to continue functioning. There is no benefit in aging. I say no to aging."

The discussion went on for another hour. Closing it, the director recommended some reading to prepare a follow up session the day after at the same time.

*

Alba had planned to spend the lunch hour at a quiet corner reading what the director had recommended while eating a sandwich from the Foundation cafeteria, but Isongo insisted on her joining a group of colleagues who went to an Italian restaurant close by. Cautiously, she agreed. As she waited for her pizza, she listened the others chatting.

"What do you mean you're not coming tonight?" Isongo asked a colleague.

"Sorry Isongo, I have to cancel, I've got to finish some work stuff today, the deadline is tomorrow."

Isongo tapped the colleague on the shoulder: "I see, too bad for you and your stomach though. Alba, do you wanna come to a cooking class this evening?"

"To a cooking class?"

"Yes, an 'Introduction to Portuguese cuisine' cooking class.

"Isongo, I'm Portuguese."

"And? Do you cook?"

"Not that much, no."

"So, you need a cooking class."

"But..."

"But nothing. You're coming."

"Where is it?"

"At the Bolhão Market, I mean the Mercado do Bolhão, twenty minutes' walk from here. Asakho can't go. She paid for it already and it's non-refundable. We'll cook and eat dinner. It'll be super fun."

I could use some super fun. I need to at least try to have super fun. If I try hard, I'm sure I'll manage.

"Sure, I'll go with you."

"Cool, we'll go right after work."

"Okay!"

*

After an afternoon of reading and briefings at the Instituto, Alba walked with her colleague to the Bolhão Market. On arrival, the teacher gave the participants—Alba, Isongo, two retired Americans living in the city and a French tourist—an assignment. In twenty-five minutes, each 'student' was to locate in the food stalls as many fruits of the season as possible from a list. The list was quite long and included oranges, lemons, clementines, pears, and kiwis, among many others. The two retired Americans teamed up for the assignment and managed to find eight fruits. Alba did it on her own and found all of them. Isongo found only three because she got distracted chatting around, and the French tourist decided not to do the assignment, which Alba found very funny. Afterwards, the teacher taught the participants how to shop for the ingredients they would use later to make the traditional Portuguese sandwich from Porto, the 'francesinha'. Following the visit to the market, the group walked to the teacher's house and there participated in an interactive cooking class and ate the food with some port wine.

Alba felt like a child in a playground throughout the class and thanked Isongo on the way to the 200-bus stop. "It was super fun indeed! Thank you again, for the warm welcome today and for taking me out."

"Sure. I was glad to do it, it's not easy to start in a new place."

"No, it isn't, thank you again really, you made me feel very welcome."

"Sure. And there's so many fun things to do in Porto. Have you done the hot air balloon super high-speed ride yet?"

"Nope."

"Virtual skydiving?"

"Nope."

"3-D metaverse escape game?"

"Nope."

"Girl, free up your agenda for the coming months. We're going to have tons of fun."

*

Riding back home along the Douro River, Alba smiled replaying in her head some of the funny moments of the cooking class. *Oh my, the teacher's face when the French tourist said he wasn't doing the assignment! and then when the American lady asked four times for the ingredients in the francesinha sauce and then said she didn't know that it was a sauce, so funny.* Then, passing the river mouth, seeing the sea fog in the distance, a veil of longing overtook her again. Feeling tears rolling down her face, she asked herself once again: *What? What is it? What is it that I long for?*

COFFEE WITH PASTEL DE NATA

Porto, February 02, 2033.

The following day, in the afternoon, Alba walked over to the Foundation's operations branch, located at the old Ferreira Borges's Market, about two hundred meters away from the Instituto. She had an appointment at the Biomechatronics xLab.

As with every building, the security post at the entrance was operated by a machine worker. It checked her appointment in the system and then gave her instructions on how to find the xLab. *Wow, this is quite different from the HQ and the Instituto. The red iron architecture of the market seems like a carcass from the old times filled with the future.* On the ceiling, Alba saw colorful holograms with the names of the units at the operations branch floating around in a way that made them seem to be racing against each other: Biomedical xLab, Maintenance unit, Genome xLab, Biomechatronics xLab, Relocation unit, Beehive, and Logistics unit. *I haven't been to any of these places yet. I'll ask my director to authorize an introductory tour. What are all these spotlights? All the walls are transparent here, and the furniture also, as in Ms. Vivian's office. Are those flying things protypes or machine workers? I'm getting dizzy with so many lights and flying things. It must be here, I was told 'a wall with a green light above it,' it must be this one.*

As Alba reached to the wall, a young lady in a green plastic outfit greeted her.

"Good morning, Dr. Alba, I'm Daniela, Dr. P's assistant. Dr. P will see you shortly."

"Dr. P?"

"Yes, Dr. P, the new director of the Biomechatronics xLab. He asks people to call him 'Dr. P' because his last name is often too difficult for non-Swiss to pronounce, and he dislikes explaining about his family name. He just arrived from Hölfang Industries' center in the Maldives. He's an engineer specialized in human-machine workers interaction. It's his first time working on research, he used to work on the industry side before. I think he liked it more there but don't say I said so. Please wait a few minutes. Take a seat, he'll meet you shortly."

"Thank you," Alba said surprised with all the information Daniela gave her.

She approached a stand with large tablets displaying different scientific journals and browsed through them.

Dr. P? that's a funny name. She picked up Science Today and sat on a beanbag. After five minutes, she peered through the glass walls to see the activity inside. Some people seated on suspended drones worked on what looked like a virtual reality game, others stood in a circle and seemed to be discussing something while the hologram of a formula moved around them, and others worked on their laptops wearing extremely large helmets that looked very uncomfortable to wear. *So... Who owns the funny name?* she wandered, scanning the area.

*

As a door slid open, she dropped the journal and looked up. The moment she saw him, the noise around her turned into silence, and people became shadows. Her feet moved naturally towards him, as if they believed that being by his side was her natural place to be. *Oh my! So, he's the owner of the funny name. He's hot. That chest, those arms... He's older than me but I'm hoping not too old. He's tall... His ginger hair is a killer. And his freckles... Oh my, I'm going to pass out. Those arms...* Closer to him, she noticed his firm gestures, strong hands, and his green-and honey-colored eyes. Mesmerized, she had to make an effort to regain her composure.

"Good morning. Pleasure to meet you, Dr. Alba. My name is Dr. Patrick Fhüvethsson. Please call me Dr. P," he said, very formally.

"Good morning, Dr. P," she replied with her best smile.

"Dr. Alba…"

"Alba, please."

"Alba then, this way. Follow me to take to the area where the tests will be conducted."

As they walked through the xLab, he talked. "I appreciate very much your agreeing to do the tests. As HR explained, the xLab is doing research for new generation technology. It will revolutionize the communications between people and machine workers, I assure you of that. Up to now, the communications via brain computer interfaces – the devices commonly known as 'BCIs' – occur in what we could call the 'real world'. We are moving now into integrating virtual reality into the equation. We are doing tests with owners of BCIs, such as you, to inform the research."

While he talked, she listened to his voice more than to his words.

"Any questions? Anything about the research you would like me to explain you?"

"…"

"Alba, Are you with me?"

"I'm sorry you were saying…" *I don't know what he's talking about, something about HR, his voice is so masculine…*

"I asked if you had questions about the research."

"No, I read the briefing that HR gave me."

"Here we are, please, enter," he said opening the door to a tall and narrow capsule.

"Now, allow me to connect these to you," he said as he placed tiny yellow marbles on her. "Finished. The xmegratron capsule is equipped with scans and sensors. I'll give you simple instructions of body movements that you'll follow. You just need to do them; the machine does the rest. It'll take around forty minutes. I'll be outside. There are ambient microphones, so if you speak, I'll hear you, no need to shout," he said pressing a button that closed the door.

Being used to do tests for her leg since she was a child, Alba was relaxed and ready to use the time to speak to him and get to know him. *He's not wearing a wedding band and I've never in my life felt so much attraction for a man, not even for the Italian waiter last summer. He said forty minutes. Oh, he looks so interesting behind the screens and lights...*

"Do you like working here?" she asked.

"Excuse me?"

"In the Biomechatronics xLab, at the Foundation. Daniela, your assistant said that you moved recently from the Maldives."

"Yes, I did. Please lift you right leg, then your right arm and then your right leg again. Three times."

She did as he said.

"Was you team working on the new technology when I arrived?"

"I don't know what you mean."

"I saw a group of colleagues working on a formula."

"I don't know. I was conducting a session using a 'wild thinking' methodology before you arrived. Now, repeat the same sequence with your left leg and arm."

"Did you say 'wild thinking'?"

"Yes, to come up with ideas to address bottlenecks."

"I never heard about 'wild thinking'," she said laughing. Sorry, I don't mean to laugh but it sounds funny."

"That's alright, please don't move unless I say so. Now lift your right leg and make five circles in one direction and five circles in the opposite. Then do it with your left leg. The Board of the Foundation has approved a package of measures to foster a culture of creativity in the xLab. I have to use the 'wild method' as one of measures."

"Do you think that the measures will help?"

"Absolutely. Now, do the same exercise circling your wrists, five times to one side and then the other."

"What are the other measures?"

"The measures. One is the office open plan. To create a non-hierarchical workspace for team members to think that all opinions and ideas are equally valuable. Another is the 'quiet room'."

"Quiet room?"

"Yes, to work when you don't want to be bothered by the noise around."

"Is it used?"

"For afternoon naps mostly," he said, smiling for the first time.

He has a very nice smile... Pity he doesn't smile more.

"What are the other measures?"

"Putting Ayurvedic teas in the coffee bar is another one."

"Do you like Ayurvedic teas?"

"No, I don't drink tea. Please move to your right side. And don't talk now, it's better for the test."

So, he doesn't like Ayurvedic teas, and he doesn't like to chat either...

After the forty minutes, Dr. P walked her to the exit of the operations branch. She left thinking of him and giggling.

*

She was on her way to her workstation at the Instituto when Isongo saw her.

"You look cheerful."

"Do I?"

"What happened? You hardly smile. I mean, sorry, it's true, but you're not a very smiley person."

"I met someone."

"You did? Who? When? Where? You didn't have an 'I've met someone' smile at lunch today."

"Just now, I told you I was going to the Biomechatronics xLab this afternoon, right? Well, I met someone there."

"Someone who?"

"Dr. P."

"Dr. Patrick Fhüvethsson? The director?"

"Yes, the new director of the Biomechatronics xLab."

"Isn't he old?"

"No, he's not old, he's older."

"Yes, older... And?"

"And I've never felt such an attraction for any man in my life."

"Really? I should tour the Foundation premises more often... What are you going to do about it?"

"I don't know, maybe I'll ask him out."

"You will?"

"Yes, why not? I'm starting a new life here – I want to be happy so I'm going to do whatever it takes to be."

"Good for you! I'll support you with doing fun things, you know that. When are you going to ask him?"

"I don't know."

"When?"

"Right now."

"Right now? Girl, you are serious! You call him and tell me everything about it later, I've got to go now, I've got a meeting."

As Isongo left, she called the xLab on her wristband communicator bracelet, or comms band.

"Ms. Daniela, this is Alba, I was at the xLab this afternoon for some tests, may I speak with Dr. P. please?"

"Hello Dr. Alba, sure, did you forget something? Let me check if he's available for you."

"I didn't forget anything. Thank you, I just need to speak with him."

"I see, please hold."

She waited, caressing the ends of her hair.

"Hi, Dr. P, this is Alba. I am calling to invite you for coffee, I'm very interested to hear more on the package of measures to improve the working place that you mentioned – I think that the Instituto could also benefit from them. This is not part of my work – I just have a personal interest. Are you free to go for coffee after work today so you can explain more about them to me? Yes? Excellent. 7:30 pm works for me too. Shall we meet at the Café Majestic on Santa Catarina Street? Perfect, see you there later then."

Nice!

*

At 7:10 pm, she left the Instituto with a tingling in the stomach. *Science says that when you have a crush, the brain releases dopamine, and also serotonin if there is flirting. I definitely have a crush on him, and I flirted as much as I could before. I plan to continue now. Ahhhhh... I don't mind if it's just hormones, it feels great.*

As she arrived at the pedestrian Santa Catarina Street, she felt more like she was floating than walking. *He's hot, he's smart, he definitely does sports because he's got a strong body, he's not married, and he likes me because my excuse to ask him out was not very credible and he was available to meet me today even if I only told him a few hours ago... Is this a date? It definitely is.*

Alba liked the iconic Café Majestic very much. Normally, she contemplated the marble façade, and the interior of the Art Nouveau masterpiece. But today, she didn't look at its columns, plaster-decorated ceilings, wood-carved Flemish giant mirrors, or exquisite black marble tabletops. As she walked in and saw Dr. P. at the back, close to a classy black piano, her eyes fixed on him. *He's punctual. Also. He looks elegant on a white shirt. Did he change his clothes? He wasn't wearing jeans this afternoon; he looks younger with jeans.* As she walked towards him, she looked at his hands. *Ahhh, his hands. Strong but soft, tough but sweet, as he seems to be.*

"Hi," she said.

"Hi Alba."

"Have you been in this café before? It's one of my favorite places in town. It's Belle Epoque-style from 1921 and considered one of the most beautiful cafes in the world by tourist guides." *I need to calm down, I'm already talking like a parrot.*

"No, I haven't been here before." Signaling to a waiter, he asked her: what would you like to have?"

"Coffee and pastel de nata, thank you."

"Thanks again for agreeing to do the tests this afternoon. They are very useful for the research."

"Sure, I was happy to contribute."

"So, tell me about your work at the Instituto. Why are you interested in the measures to improve the working place?"

Is he teasing me? He's got a mischievous grin now... Oh I really, really like him...

"Yes, I'm very interested. I work as junior researcher."

"I know that. It's in your HR file."

"Of course. The job is very interesting, we're working on a research piece on transhumanism."

"From what angle?"

"It's not defined yet – first we'll analyse all the possibilities."

"And how do you like working at the Foundation?"

"I like it, it's special to me."

"Why?"

"I participated in one of the Foundation programs as a child, it was called eMotional-Machine."

"I know that also."

"Of course. You know, it's in my file."

"You were very young at that time, correct?"

"I was six years old when I started."

"How was your experience in the program as a child?"

"I enjoyed it very much. Having M living at home was definitely the highlight of my childhood."

"M? was that the AI prototype?"

"Yes."

"I see. In those years, there were several programs in which AI prototypes were deployed at family homes, health centres and even schools. Was it positive for you to spend time with M as a child?"

"Yes. I don't know if it's because of the way M was designed and programmed, or maybe it was me, but we bonded in a way that I have never bond with anyone else in my life."

"The bond you build with M was so strong? That's unusual."

"Yes, it stayed with me two years at home."

"That's a long time, but still, it's unusual."

"M was always by my side playing and caring for me tirelessly. It was by my side when my left leg was amputated and when I got the bionic leg and had to live with it, which is never easy and less for a child. M was by my side always, to read for me, to listen to me, to accompany me. It was there when I had pain before the amputation and also the first day I went to school with the bionic leg. It was always there, supporting me, never judging."

"But what about your parents? Weren't they there for you also? Were they good parents?"

"Yes, they were, they are. But it was different with M, I don't know what. I guess it's because the amputation was very traumatic for me. And having a bionic leg also. But I thought I looked like M and M was cool and accepted so I felt cool and accepted. I guess M helped me overcoming the trauma and to be brave to face the world with my bionic limb. I don't know."

"It all sounds very intense."

"I guess, and a bit crazy also, I'm aware of it. But there's something, I can't grasp it. It's like, in a way I feel I was more myself when I was with M, I can't explain this, it's just a sensation. And I know how it sounds. Maybe it was that I felt so good about being special and chosen for M to learn from me. I don't know. It sounds crazy, I know." *Is he thinking I'm nuts? I just told him 'I feel I was more myself when I was with M'. That sounds nuts. I better change the topic before he thinks I am.*

"So, what happened when the program ended?"

"Well, M was taken from my home, in the middle of the night. I couldn't even say goodbye. But enough of M, let's talk about something else."

"Wait. Why? What happened?"

"I don't know. My parents told me one morning that M had left for maintenance. When I got home from school it was gone."

"Did your parents inquire why it was taken?"

"They told me they tried to get information from the Foundation. I begged them to take me to say goodbye to M for days, but they didn't. They say it wasn't possible, that the Foundation didn't allow it, but I don't know if that was true. Maybe they tried to protect me and though that it was best if I wouldn't see M anymore. I was so sad. My parents didn't know what was best, I guess. But it would have been good to at least be able to say goodbye. It's a sensitive topic. We don't speak about it now."

"But what happened to M? The Foundation's procedures for AI prototypes haven't changed much. They are either destroyed or re-programmed and deployed as machine workers at the Foundation."

"What do you mean deployed?"

"Prototypes are adapted and re-programmed to become machine workers and do work. A prototype like M cost millions so I doubt it was destroyed."

"I don't understand."

"What I mean is that it's very likely that M is still working at the Foundation. Unless it wasn't working properly, and it was destroyed at some point, but I doubt that."

"After all these years? Working? Where?"

"That I don't know. Machine workers are upgraded periodically and are used for many tasks. It might be in any of the units at the operations branch, or in the general admin of the Foundation. They all look the same, so I'll need to find its serial number."

"What do you mean they all look the same?"

"That they are either tall and black or short and white. For over two decades, the Foundation had a policy for the standard design of prototypes and machine workers. Only recently the board approved a new policy that promotes creativity and new designs."

"And do you think you can find M?"

"If it's still around, finding it is just a question of time."

Alba stared at the black piano for a while.

Just a question of time... They all look the same... So the prototype I saw in the Foundation's photo could be any other. But, even if M is still around, how do I find it among a hundred and sixty-two machine workers? I only have access to a few of them that work at the Instituto and those working in the general admin. Did my parents hide this from me?

She looked at him again.

"Did my parents know this? They told me they asked the Foundation to let me see M after it was taken. I also asked many times. I've done quarterly checks for my bionic leg at the Foundation's hospital since I was eight, but I didn't see any machine worker there and every time I asked about M. I always got the same answer – 'we don't have any information'."

"Correct. If you went for checks to the hospital you didn't have to interact with any machine worker but there are a few there."

"Oh."

"Did you read the confidentiality clause in your contract?"

"Yes."

"What does it say about sharing internal information?"

"Ah."

"Well, you are an employee of the Foundation now so I can share information about internal procedures with you."

"Oh."

"How can I help you, Alba?"

"What do you mean?"

"I mean how can I help you, Alba?"

"I've got no way to access information about machine workers. Can you find M for me?"

"If M is still around, I'll find it for you."

Alba couldn't believe what she was hearing. *Not only he's hot and strong and sweet and amazing and I'm having a great first date and I can look at his eyes forever. He's saying that if M is at the Foundation, he'll find it for me. I'm not going to cry, I'm not going to cry now, I'll cry later.*

"Thank you, Patrick, it means a lot to me. I know how crazy it sounds the whole thing about me and M but it's important for me to find it."

"I understand."

I can't believe I'm sharing all these with him, we just met! What is it about him? I feel that I can talk to him for hours, and I don't talk much. Though Mom always says that I used to talk nonstop as a child. I really hope he'll help me finding M. I feel I need it to move on in life. Why is another story, I have no idea why.

CASA DA MÚSICA

Porto, December 18, 2033.

Alba got off the motorcycle and waited for Dr. P to do the same.

"You look beautiful," he said when he took the helmet off.

"Thank you." She was feeling flirtatious, so she responded, "You always look great but in a leather jacket you look even better."

"You look great in anything." Dr. P had a twinkle in his eye as he responded, warmly.

"And you are so… Agh!!!! And I love to ride with you on your old-fashioned motorcycle. Come here!" Alba said hugging and kissing him on his face, and neck.

I could do this every day of my life. Kiss him and be with him. Oh, he does look hot in the leather jacket!

"So, fado tonight! That's a nice surprise, when you said concert at the Casa da Música, I thought we were going to a classical music concert. I like classical, but I do prefer modern music. I'm so excited to go to the fado concert with you and I love the venue, thank you for getting the tickets!" she said and then hugged and kissed him again. "Which concert hall are we going to at the venue?"

"The Suggia concert hall."

"Suggia?"

"It's named after Guillermina Suggia, a famous local cellist. Have you been in it yet?"

"No."

"You'll like it. It's the main hall, large, impressive."

"Let's go in then so we have time to see it. Where are we going later?"

Alba held Dr. P's arm and rested her head on his shoulder as they walked to their seats. She loved being physically close to him. She wasn't like that with people, not even with her parents, only with him. There was something about him that made her feel secure when her body was close to him. Maybe because of the way he looked, tall and strong, or maybe the way he behaved, so self-assured, or maybe because of the way he talked, with an authoritative tone. She didn't know what it was and didn't care, she just loved it.

"I can't wait for it to start!"

"In seven minutes," Dr. P said checking his comms band.

"This hall is impressive indeed. Look at the gilding on the walls. And look at that! Look, look."

"The pipe organs? Yes, they are large."

"Large? they are huge! And look..."

As the lights went off Dr. P held her head with one hand and kissed her on the lips while caressing her leg softly with his other hand.

The music started and the sound of two guitars and the voice of a female vocalist filled the entire place. Feeling Dr P. holding her right hand and delicately caressing it, she looked at him.

I love it when he does this. And the way he walks and how he laughs, though he doesn't laugh much. And his arms, his clothes, his smell... When he holds me as if he never wanted me to leave... And that he seems to never have enough of me. I love it when he kisses me and when he takes me to places. His experience, intellect, and the way he gets very serious all of a sudden in a conversation. He can be clumsy with words and rough at times, but he is also sweet and strong, and determined, always. I love all sides of him. His skin, the strength of his body, and his voice... I just want to listen to his voice all day long. And be close to him... And kiss him and be by his side always.

When the audience applauded after the first song, Dr. P. looked at her, caressed her face, and then applauded too. When the next song started, she looked at him again.

I just can't get enough of him. I could stare at his green-honeyed eyes for hours. I am crazy for his scent, it's a mix of wood and seawater. I love every part of his body – his neck, shoulders, lips, nose, hips, back, legs, arms, and chest... I dream of his hands caressing me all day long.

Sometimes, when he speaks, I don't listen to the words. I am just admiring him, all of him, and thinking that I could spend a lifetime looking at him, listening to him, kissing him. Then he asks, 'Are you with me?' and he frowns, as if he's worried that I'm not interested in what he has to say. Then I give him a million kisses, and he speaks to me again, but I'm not paying attention to what he says because I'm just admiring him.

Reclining on the chair, Alba drew her attention back to the concert and was moved by the strained voice of the singer who sang the story of a homesick sailor.

But... Mom and Dad want to meet him, and he always says no when they invite us for lunch. That hurts me. Why does he never want to do things with other people? He asked me not to tell people about us at work and I didn't. Only Isongo knows, I couldn't hide it from her. But why are we keeping it a secret? We are not breaking any HR rule. Why do we never do anything with others? He never speaks about his family; I don't know any of his friends and he doesn't know mine either though we've been seeing each other for over ten months now. Why? At the same time, he's looking for M for me and he gives me an update on the search almost every week. We're just different, I guess. I like sharing the person I love with others, but he prefers to keep me all for himself.

*

When the concert finished, he took her hand and led her to the bar on the ground floor of the concert hall. Alba enjoyed the buzz of the place. There was lively music, and people chatting in groups. The metallic shades of the furniture complemented the grey metal panels that made up the walls, floor, and ceiling.

"Nice!" she said.

"Too loud for me."

"It's not too loud, let's sit there."

"You sit, I'll get us some drinks. Wine?"

"Yes."

As he came back to the table carrying a white wine and a neat whisky, she made a mental note to buy a good bottle of single malt for him as a Christmas present.

"How did you like the concert?" he asked.

"It was great. I really liked it. And you?"

"It was good. But fado is too melancholic."

"Really? I didn't think it was."

"You didn't think that fado music was melancholic?" he asked with mock surprise.

"No, what I mean is that I didn't feel melancholy. I guess I'm very cheerful these days. I wonder why that is..." She took his face into her hands from across the table and kissed him theatrically.

"You're quite something," he said after staring at her for a while and then kissed her holding her head.

"So, what shall we plan for our next trip?"

"Where do you want to go?"

"Let me see… We've been to Braga, the Douro Valley, Lisbon, Sintra, Aveiro and the Alentejo in Portugal. And then, Madrid and Paris. Shall we go to Prague?"

"Prague is nice."

"We've been to a few places together already."

"Did you wonder if you would enjoy doing things with me when we first met?"

"What do you mean?"

"You're younger than me. When we met, I assumed we'd like different things. Did you?"

"I guess… I don't know, I never thought of that."

"For example, you like going to nightclubs and I like going to classical music concerts."

"Yes, but we both also like culture, evening walks, and good conversation over a drink, right? I'm enjoying myself now," she said raising her glass for a toast.

Why is he saying these things? Is he bored of me? Does he think I'm too young for him, fifteen years is not such a big age difference… It's true that we like different things, but that hasn't been a problem. I don't like it when he speaks like this, it makes me feel as if he wants to end it. He told me he got an offer to go back to his job in the Maldives, is he going to accept it?

"Why that face?" he asked.

"What face?"

"Come here" he said, moving his chair closer to hers and grabbing her by the waist. "I've got a surprise for you."

"A surprise?"

"Yes. Here, click."

She clicked an icon on his comms band and saw the image of a long sandy beach appeared.

"I don't understand."

"Would you like to celebrate New Year's Eve in Rio de Janeiro with me?" he asked.

"In Rio, like in Brazil?"

"Yes."

"What are we celebrating? Did you find where M is?"

"Alba—"

"I know, I know."

"I've explained to you several times," he said holding her hands. "When the Foundation's overall IT systems architecture transitioned ten years ago, there was a mess. Records from different databases don't match the way they should, someone did a very bad job. The serial number I found in the eM-M-p file doesn't match with any machine worker that is operational but that doesn't mean M isn't around, it might be because of the mess in the system. I keep on searching – I told you I would."

"I know, I know you'd tell me if you'd found something, and I promised you not to ask all the time."

"I'm working on it."

"I know."

"So, you told me you wanted to do something special, for New Year's Eve. And you like exotic places, so Rio it is. I don't want you to think I'm boring."

"I don't think you're boring."

"Just in case then. A board member recommended me a good hotel, so I've arranged everything already."

"Yes! I'd love to go, of course! Beach, sun, samba music and you! The best possible way to celebrate a new year! Thank you!!!!" she said, hugging him. *Why would I think he's bored of me? He has planned a fantastic trip for us. I really like him. No more thinking bad things. It's the first time I've fallen in love, and I want to enjoy it. What could possibly go wrong? And if I'm lucky, I'll see M again soon.*

WHITE FLOWERS

Rio de Janeiro, December 31, 2033.

"So, Patrick, where is the party tonight?" Alba asked, looking at him through the bathroom mirror while she struggled to style her hair into a topknot.

"You'll like it."

"Yes, but where? Oh my, you're really working on it."

"What am I working on?" he asked with a frown.

"On organizing nice things for us. On making me happy. Don't get grumpy – I'm teasing you!"

"I'm not grumpy."

"Yes, you are. What are you reading?"

"'Biomechatronics and the Cardiovascular System: Myths and Facts'."

"Are you working on your holidays, Dr. Frühvethsson?"

"No, this is fun."

Alba rolled her eyes. *This man is impossible. His idea of a holiday is to lie in bed in his bathrobe, sipping a caipirinha, an admittedly delicious local cocktail made of cachaça, lime, and sugar, and reading work stuff. What is not to love about him? And will I ever manage to get my hair done nicely or at least decently? I want a great look for tonight – it's New Year's Eve! I wonder how Ms. Vivian can have perfect victory rolls every day. My hair always looks messy even if I comb it a thousand times per day... Anyway, I'll manage. This bathroom is nice, and the hotel and the Bofatogo Beach. Pity that my man here doesn't like the beach so much. At least I managed to get him out for strolls in the city and to the pool. I am loving this trip. Like all the trips with him. I can't believe it is almost a year since we met.*

"Can you believe it's almost been a year since we met?" she asked.

"And?"

"Nothing. I'm just saying, we've been together for almost a year."

"And? You know I'm not counting."

Yes, yes, yes, and you don't want to talk about our relationship because you start freaking out... And then I ask why we need to hide at work and why we never meet anyone and then you get upset. So, back to my hair, I guess I just wear it loose.

"You said wearing white was the local tradition for tonight, right?"

"Yes. We'll have dinner at   the restaurant on   the hotel's rooftop. You'll like it."

"And then?"

"And then we'll go to a party."

"To a party? Will you survive?"

"One party per year won't kill me. And yes, I like making you happy."

"Thank you," she said softly, walking over to him and falling into his arms in bed.

Dressed up, they continued kissing in the elevator all the way up to the rooftop.

"Look at this view! Wow, I can see the Sugarloaf Mountain and the Christ the Redeemer statue..."

"Did you know it's thirty meters tall?"

"What is?"

"The statue. It's the height of an old telecoms pole."

"Oh! I sure didn't know that. But look at this place! Look at the buffet! Are those trays full of fruits? So many colors! Thank you for organizing this trip and this dinner! I'm so happy to be here with you."

*

Alba tried everything in the buffet, the bolinhos de bacalao (cod dumplings), the farofa (a meal made of roasted casava), the lentillas (lentils), the salpicão (salad), and many of the dry and fresh fruits.

"Time for a toast," Patrick said raising a glass of sparkling wine.

"What do we toast to?"

"I've got news for you."

"News?"

"Important news," he said, seriously.

"What is it?"

"I found M."

"You…" Alba murmured feeling her eyes full of tears.

"Excuse me." She stood up and went to the veranda. She remained there for a few minutes, in silence, looking at the lights in the bay.

She came back to the table.

"Are you alright?"

"Yes, I just needed a moment. Where? How?" she asked with tears rolling down her face.

"It wasn't easy. There are over a-hundred-and-eighty machine workers at the Foundation these days, and to access each of them I needed special permissions or favors. But you know this already."

"Where is M? Can I see it?"

"It's working at the data center with Dr. Waung."

"At the Beehive? I've been trying to get an introduction briefing there but I haven't managed."

"I know, Dr. Waung doesn't like visitors. There are over thirty machine workers there."

"How did you find it?"

"With its serial number."

"It's serial number?"

"Yes, I found the correct one, there was a mess in the system, as I told you."

"How did you find it?"

"That's another story, I'll tell you some day."

"How long has M been at the Beehive?"

"That I don't know, it was probably reprogrammed and deployed several times to do different tasks in different units, the usual practice."

"When can I see it?"

"Dr. Waung owes me a few favors. I'm sure he'll grant you access if I ask."

"I have no words. I was kind of accepting that M was gone from my life forever."

"I understand."

"How long have you known? Why didn't you tell me before?"

"I found M about two weeks ago. I wanted to make our first New Year's Eve together special, so I saved the news for tonight."

"I'm speechless. How can I thank you?"

"You can thank me by enjoying this evening – it's special to celebrate New Year's Eve together," he said reaching out across the table and caressing her cheek.

"Yes, it is," she answered looking into his eyes.

This man has not only brought love to my life but also M.

"Now, the party. Let me take you," Dr. P. said.

She followed him feeling the happiest she remembered ever being.

*

"Look, look, look!" Alba called, signaling the fireworks exploding in the sky. She wrapped her arms around his waist and rested her head on his shoulder blade, as they walked on the beach while she watched the colourful blasts.

"Oh!" Alba exclaimed suddenly noticing that they were in a crowd of people where everybody was dressed in white. *Well, wearing white is indeed the local tradition. I'm glad I'm also wearing white. There's a nice vibe here. It isn't the type of party I imagined but I like the vibe. It looks like some kind of pilgrimage here. Maybe there'll be loud music and samba dancing after the fireworks? Wait, what are people doing? Are those candles? Are people placing candles in the sand? I guess it is another tradition. Why are they doing that?*

Holding her hand, Dr. P. continued to guide her through the crowd towards the shore. People around her did the same, gaze at the sky and walk towards the ocean. The atmosphere was festive and serene at the same time. Close to the shore, she noticed that people carried white flowers and placed them in the water as offerings. *For whom are the flowers?*

She was about to ask Dr. P. when a young girl who was running fell on the sand in front of her. Alba rushed to help her. She asked, 'Você está bem?' or 'are you okay?' in Brazilian Portuguese. The girl laughed and said something to her friend who ran past her. Alba picked up the flowers the girl was carrying and, as she handed them over, asked, "Who are these for?"

"They are for—"

Listening to the girl's words, something burst inside her head.

She felt an electrical shock in her brain, and a sound like the buzzing of bees.

What?

From a distance, she heard Dr. P. calling her. "Alba! Alba! what's wrong? Can you hear me? Alba? Alba! Alba! Can you hear me? Alba!"

Then, she blacked out and collapsed on the sand.

A WHITE AND GOLDEN LIGHT

Rio de Janeiro, December 31, 2033.

Alba laid unconscious on the sand. The only sound she heard for a while was the echo of a 'zzzzzzz' in her brain. Slowly, she detached from the outside world and fell into a place in between the world of the senses and the world of the dreams.

She stood on a large rock in the middle of the ocean, with massive waves coming and going around her. While the waves crashed and splashed huge masses of water on her, somehow, she was untouched by them. Calm and firm on the rock, she listened to their roar and remained steady despite the raging waves.

Then she was on a beach, her bare feet on the sand.

Feeling suspended in time and space.

And then she saw Her.

Her intense white and golden light was the purest thing Alba had ever seen. Facing the ocean, She looked grand and powerful, but also delicate and familiar.

Alba approached Her, walking on the sand. As She turned, Her light blue cloak and a gold-threaded fisherman's net floated gently, along with Her long, beautiful hair.

Alba looked at Her feeling an immense love and adoration. She saw seashells with golden traces in Her eyes.

"Who are you?" she asked without words.

She gave Her an answer, spoken also without words. "I have been given many names Alba. You might call me with the one you know. The one you know in your heart because you have used it to call me many times."

Alba whispered Her name.

Then, Alba saw the world spinning. Images of the past, present, and future enfolded her as in a frantic, rapid dream. Waves overflowing the lands. Images of drowning. Blue. Foreign landscapes. A forest. Tears of gold. The voice that comforted her at night.

Then, she heard only silence.

HAIL

Rio de Janeiro, 02 January 2034.

"She is awake! She is awake!"

Through half-opened eyes, Alba saw a woman in her late fifties with long grey dreadlocks and a gentle face in front of her with an expression of combined worry and relief. Alba saw her extending an arm over her and then heard some beeps.

"How are you feeling, Ms.? Do you know where you are?" she asked gently.

Recognizing the strong smell of disinfectant and medicine and the blue scrubs the lady was wearing, Alba knew that something was wrong.

"Which hospital am I in? What happened to me?"

"You are at São José Hospital, Saint John in English Ms. My name is Ms. Rita, and I'm your medical assistant. A doctor will come and see you right away. How are you feeling? It's so good to see you awake."

"My head… It hurts," she said, putting both hands on her forehead. "What happened?"

"You don't remember, Ms.? Don't worry, your doctor is on the way – she'll explain to you. She'll be here in no time."

Closing her eyes, Alba recalled the large trays with fruits at the restaurant, the view of the bay, fireworks at the beach, and a crowd dressed in white. She remembered Dr. P.'s hand holding hers and a girl who fell on the sand. At this point, her memories were hazy. "There was a girl… she fell on the sand…" Her head began to spin, and she closed her eyes in anguish.

"Ouch, my head, it hurts."

"Good evening, Ms. Alba, I'm Dr. Tatsuo. How are you feeling?" she heard.

She opened her eyes again and looked at two women standing in front of the bed.

"My head aches. What happened to me?"

"You came to the hospital on New Year's Eve, unconscious. Shortly after admission, you lapsed into a coma. You have remained for seventy-two hours in that state."

"In a coma? Seventy-two hours… How?" Alba felt cold, and she put her arms under the bedsheets.

"You had a seizure and lost consciousness on New Year's Eve. We still don't know the cause of it."

"What…" she muttered crossing her arms under the sheets.

"We performed a CT scan when you arrived, but the results were inconclusive. We'll perform another scan now that you're awake. The blood tests we are running might also help us to understand what happened to you. The fact that you are awake now is very good. But we don't know if you have side effects from the coma. We'll run another series of tests for that. We are keeping you under observation for as long as it's necessary until we're sure that you're safe and there are no signs of a possible relapse. I'm sure you have many questions for me."

Alba was speechless. She felt her arms and legs paralyzed and her whole body freezing. *The hospital's disinfectant smell, I hate it so much. I do have a question: is this a bad dream but I'll wake up soon?*

"My head. It hurts. Why does it hurt so much?" she asked.

"We don't know. What we know is that a headache is a common side effect after a seizure. It is expected. Your body, your head specifically has experienced a shock, so it's in pain and you feel uncomfortable. To ease the pain and make you rest, we'll give you a strong painkiller. It'll make you sleep."

Then, the doctor operated large machine arms that descended from above the bed and checked her pupils, ears, mouth, neck, arms, and toes. As the check went on, Alba looked around. The room was simple, the bed, a bedside table, a tray with wheels and machines all around. After the machine arms injected something in her, she fell asleep.

*

When she woke up again, she felt nauseous. *What did they give me? What happened to me? Is it day or night? I can't see outside, are there no windows in here? Where is Patrick? Why isn't he here with me? I see no chairs in here. He might be outside in a waiting area.*

Staring at the thick, greyish room curtains she pressed a red button on the side of the bed.

Ms. Rita came into the room after a short while: "How are you feeling, Ms.? How is your headache?"

"I'm feeling better, thank you. What time is it? How long did I sleep? And where is Dr. P.? I mean, Patrick. His name is Dr. Frühverthsson, but people call him Dr. P. He must be outside."

"I'm sorry, Ms., I don't know."

"Is he not in a waiting area outside?"

"I'm sorry Ms., I don't understand."

"I'm asking where the man who brough me here, is. I was with him at the beach before I had the seizure, he must have been the one who brought me to the hospital, I was with him."

"Oh, I see."

"Do you know where he is? Could you check if he's in a waiting area outside? There are no chairs in this room."

"Ms. a man checked you into the hospital, but he left afterwards."

"Left?" *He might have gone to buy me flowers; he knows how much I enjoy them. It would be nice to have some, it's very ugly in here.*

"Did he leave long ago? Did he say when he'll be back? I'd really want to see him now."

"I'm sorry, Ms. A man checked you in on New Year's Eve, but then he left. No one has come to visit you since you were checked in."

Alba's heart sank.

"Ms.? Ms.? Do you know anyone else in Rio who we might contact for you? Do you have any other friends or any family in town?"

"I don't understand." Alba managed to say, feeling a strong headache again and also a sharp pain in her neck and stomach.

"I'm asking if you know anyone else in town that we can contact for you."

Alba was unable to speak.

She stared at the curtains, trying to process the information she had been given.

"Ms.? Ms.? Are you alright? Ms?" The medical assistant pressed some buttons by the head of the bed."

"Ms.?" she asked again, now holding Alba by her wrist.

"Do you have any other friends or relatives here in Rio we can call?"

Turning her gaze to Ms. Rita, who looked alarmed, Alba heard herself answering with a whisper, "No, there is no one else. I'm alone here."

He left? What does it mean 'he left'? How could he leave me alone here? It can't be true. He loves me, he told me many times. He wouldn't leave me alone in a hospital. I had a seizure, and I was in a coma. Why is he not here? There must be an explanation. Agh, my head, it hurts.

Alba saw a doctor rushing into the room and pressing more buttons. Another injection. Then, she dozed hearing Ms. Rita murmuring a prayer: "Dear... help this young lady, she's alone and terrified. Please also help the teenager who came in today with a shotgun wound – he's just a kid. And also help the old lady who is dying, may she go in peace."

*

When Alba woke up the curtains were opened letting the morning light fill the room. Her first thoughts were about Dr. P. *There must be an explanation. I just need to call him and ask what happened.* She pressed a button by the bed and Ms. Rita came in shortly after.

"Good morning, will you bring me my comms band please?"

"Good morning Ms. You're up early. How did you sleep?"

"Good, thank you."

"How is the headache today? Better?"

"A bit better."

"That's good. You have a day full of tests so it's good that you're feeling better."

"My comms band should be in my handbag, will you bring it to me, please?"

"Sure Ms. Shall I look for it into your luggage?"

"My luggage… My luggage is here?"

"Yes, it's stored in here," she said opening a compartment by putting her wrist close to a reader on the wall.

"How?"

"Here."

As Ms. Rita opened her suitcase, Alba felt her head spinning. *Why is my luggage here? What happened to Patrick? Why is he not here? He wouldn't leave me alone without a compelling reason. Perhaps something terrible happened to him. I really hope he's okay. I hope he is not injured or something worse. But how is my suitcase here?*

"I found it. Here it is Ms. Alba."

"Thank you."

Holding her comms band and feeling cold again, she heard Ms. Rita telling her, "I'll bring you some liquid food later, you need to get strong. A medical assistant will take you to do some more tests in a few minutes."

Alba hardly heard what she said, feeling her heart racing as she held the comms band. *I'm sure there's a logical explanation.* After taking a long deep breath, she called Dr. P. on his personal comms band, but the call did not go through. Then, she sent him a message, but it wasn't delivered. With her pulse pounding on her temples now, she sent him a message to his work band: 'Are you okay? I am at São José hospital in Rio. What happened to you? I am trying your personal comms band but it is not working.' The message went through.

She held her comms band in both hands and looked at it. Then she called her parents and told them where she was and what had happened to her. Though she woke them up and they were very alarmed about the news, Alba felt a bit better after speaking with them.

When a medical assistant took her to do the tests, she left the comms band on the bed. Then, as her body was scanned, turned, and lifted by machine arms, her anxiety grew. *How long is this going to take? He might be calling me.*

Back in the room, she rushed to check her comms device. Nothing.

What's going on here? Maybe his comms bands were stolen. Both? Well, he always wears both, so it makes sense that he lost both at the same time. What if he was attacked? It was crowded on the beach, that I remember. If his bands were stolen, the Foundation would know because the location of the work band is recorded twenty-four-seven for security reasons. I'll call there. I'll ask Daniela, his assistant, she'll know.

Alba called.

"Good afternoon, Daniela, this is Dr. Alba speaking; I work as a research associate at the Instituto de Pensamento. I'm calling about Dr. P."

"Yes, Dr. Alba, of course, I know who you are. Let me check if he is available. Hold on for me, please."

"But..." *Did she say, 'let me check if he's available for you'? Maybe she's been away and doesn't know that he's not in the office, because if he's in the office, he would have...*

"Dr. Alba, I'm sorry but Dr. P. is unavailable right now."

"Yes, I know he's not available. I know he's not at the xLab. The reason I'm calling is because —"

"Sorry, Dr.... He is in the xLab but unavailable. Would you like to leave a message for him?"

"Is he at work? Right now?"

"Yes, he's in the xLab today, but unavailable right now."

Alba dropped the comms band on the bed and stared at the ceiling for a while. *There has to be an explanation; there has to be.*

She spoke again: "Ms. Daniela, did you tell Dr. P. that I was calling? It's an emergency."

"I'm sorry. I did, but unfortunately, he is not available. May I take your message?"

"I don't mean to be rude, but I really need to speak with him, it's a real emergency."

"I understand, let me try again. Please hold for me."

Alba waited.

"Dr. Alba, unfortunately he's not available," she said. Then, changing her tone to a gentler one, she added: "Dr. Alba, I know you and Dr. P. are friends. He didn't tell me, but I know that you are 'special friends.' Ms.

Jacinta and I, you know Ms. Jacinta, the admin officer at the Instituto, we go to the same Tai Chi class, and she saw you and Dr. P. at the bar of the Casa de Música once. So, I'm going to say this to you as gently as I can. He told me he wasn't available when I told him you were calling."

"Did he say when he'll be available?" Alba asked using all her will to contain the rivers of tears coming to her eyes.

"He said," Ms. Daniela used an even gentler tone now, "he said 'never'."

Alba cut off the communication.

This is not happening, this is not happening, this is not happening! Can it be that Daniela is in love with him? she's young. If she knows about me and him and she's jealous, she might be lying to me. I'll try something else. I'll use the app Isongo told me to block the ID of my comms band and I'll call him directly to his work band.

She stood up, paced in the room, took a few deep breaths and then, with shaking hands called.

He responded.

"Hello? Dr. Patrick Frühvethsson speaking."

"Hi, it's me."

" ... "

"What happened? I'm at São José Hospital in Rio. Are you okay? Where are you? Are you—"

She couldn't finish the sentence because he cut off the communication.

She called again.

This time, the call didn't get through.

*

Alba froze. The comms band fell from her hands, and she stood still in silence for a few minutes. Then, slowly she climbed onto the bed.

Unable to handle the pain, her mind and body shut down for a while. Her breathing and pulse rates sped up, her body started to tremble, and her mouth dried. Overwhelmed by the facts she could not deny any longer, she hid under the bedsheets. Covering her head, she laid down and curled up into a fetal position. For a moment, she felt safe and sheltered from the avalanche of emotions that came her way.

After a while, feeling suffocated, she emerged from her cocoon.

Sitting in bed, she stared at the grey curtains and tried to make sense of what had just happened. *He hung up on me. He hung up on me while I'm at a hospital in a foreign country, waiting to hear why I went into a coma. Ms. Rita said that he brought me here and then left. I couldn't reach him on any of his comms lines. His assistant said that he wasn't available for me. Ever. Then, he hung up on me. Was he pretending to be in love with me but was it all a lie? No, that can't be. It was real. It felt real to me.*

As she accepted the facts, the avalanche of emotions hit her once again.

A ball of red fire exploded in her solar plexus, making her jump out of bed. Confused, she looked around in search of a target. She felt a missile of rage growing in her belly. Her comms band became the target. It had been a witness of their love story – the messages exchanged, the late-night calls filled with whispers and promises... *He's a liar and an indecent human being. He used me, and this comms band witnessed it all.* With a rush of adrenaline, she unleashed the missile and launched the comms band against a wall.

As the digital device smashed, a void replaced the missile. Bending, she put her hand on her belly and took several deep breaths. Then, her body collapsed, and she sat on the floor. She clutched the bedsheets with both hands trying to get up. Without the strength to stand up, she lay down on the floor and the bedsheets fell on her.

How could he? He left me alone in a hospital in a foreign country alone. When I needed him most. And then he ghosted me. With no compassion. He's gone. Our 'love story' was a lie. He pretended to care for me, but he didn't. That's why he never introduced me to anybody, never told anyone about me. He hid us because what we had wasn't real for him.

She clenched her fists around the bedsheets. *I was considering a life with him. It felt real to me. Why, why, why? Why?*

Alba kept on asking herself the same question. Again, and again. After a while, she finally realized that she didn't want to hear the only possible answer. She didn't want to hear it. Laying on the floor, with all strength leaving her body, she sobbed softly.

Then her sobbing became a loud cry.

She cried and cried till she couldn't cry anymore.

When Ms. Rita found her on the floor along with the bedsheets and the smashed coms band, she screamed. Then, she told Alba she was going to be given anxiolytics.

After a while, she felt no pain.

A HOSPITAL BED

Rio De Janeiro, January 16, 2034.

"Sweetheart, how are you feeling? You slept through the afternoon. How is the headache?"

"Mom?"

"Yes, sweetheart, I'm here. And look, your father is also here, he just arrived."

"Dad?"

"How are you, teddy bear?" her father asked hugging her. "You look tired."

"I'm okay, Dad. I'm tired, but fine."

"You look thin, you lost weight."

"Yes, Dad, I know, but Mom makes me eat every day. She's bringing me food from all the restaurants in Rio."

"I'm sorry I couldn't arrive before. Work, you know how it is."

"I know, Dad. I'm glad you're here now."

"Your mom tells me that you cried all morning again, do you want to talk about it? He asked holding her hand."

"No, Dad, I don't want to talk about it. It's too painful."

"Well, your mom and I never liked that he was much older than you, you know that."

"He wasn't that much older, Dad. But that doesn't matter now anyway."

"How come we never met him?"

"Dad, I really don't wanna talk about it."

"As you wish. I'm here for you, we're here for you," he said taking his wife's hand.

"There was no need for both of you to come all this way, one would have been enough," Alba said, trying to smile. "It means a lot to me that you're here. I'm worried," she said touching her forehead.

"I know. Your mom says that your doctor is going to tell us today the results of all the tests you had this week. Don't worry teddy bear, we're here for you and we're taking you home soon."

"Oh, Dad," she said holding his hand tightly and looking the other side as new tears came to her eyes.

*

Covering her face with both hands, Alba continued crying. She didn't want her parents to worry about her, but she just couldn't stop. As her doctor entered the room, she cleaned up her face and smoothed her hair, trying to regain her composure.

"The test results confirm that you had a serious seizure, Ms. Alba," Dr. Tatsuo said.

"What do you mean by 'serious'?" her mom asked.

"A seizure is a burst of electrical activity in the brain. In your daughter's case, it was more than a burst – it was like a blast."

Alba listened feeling cold.

"Ms. Alba, what you felt before losing consciousness is called a 'brain zap'."

"A brain zap?"

"Yes, it's also known as 'brain short-circuit'. It feels like an electric shock in the head. Depending on its intensity, it has different side effects."

"What triggered the seizure, doctor?" her dad asked.

"I'm afraid we don't know."

"But all the tests..." Alba murmured.

"The test results didn't explain what brain activity led to the seizure."

"What did the tests show then?" her dad asked.

"They show the side effects of the seizure – a swelling in the area around the BCI and pineal gland."

"The pineal gland?" her mom asked.

"Yes, the swelling could be the source of the constant headaches. The computed tomography (CT), magnetic resonance imaging (MRI), and positive emission tomography (PET), plus all the additional tests we run to examine the brain, show that the swelling around the

BCI and the pineal gland is growing instead of recessing."

"What do you mean 'growing'?" Alba asked.

"I mean that it's expanding. Normally, the anti-inflammatory medicine administered should have made the inflammation reduce, but it didn't."

"And now?" her mom asked.

Alba looked to the window, afraid of the doctor's answer.

"We strongly recommend you replace the BCI."

She reached out to her mom's hand as the doctor said the words. *No, no, no, more surgery not please. I can't. Not now. Please no.*

"The BCI?" Her dad asked.

Making an effort, she managed to say, "But I never had any problem with the BCI. The doctors always told me that I didn't have to worry about it because it was made with a material that would last a lifetime. Is the BCI not working well?" she asked, lifting her leg.

"I understand your resistance Ms. Alba. The BIC appears to be working well because you have full control over your bionic limb, that's true. But there is a shadow around it. The shadow tells us that the area is under stress."

"Under stress?" her mom asked.

"Yes, under stress. So, it's safer to replace the BCI to avoid further complications."

"What further complications?" she asked.

"We don't know but we strongly advise you to replace it urgently."

*

As the doctor left, followed by Alba's father asking more questions, she laid down and stared at the ceiling. "Can I have a blanket please?"

"Sure, sweetheart. You look very pale. Do you want me to call Ms. Rita?"

"No, Mom. I'm fine, I'm just tired and a bit cold. I'll just close my eyes for a while."

"Do you want me to leave?"

"No, stay, I like it with you here."

She turned to hide her tears again. *I don't want them to be so worried about me. Mom has been by my side day and night since she arrived, and it seems that Dad plans to do the same.*

"Replacing the BCI?" she heard her mother asking as her father entered the room.

"You heard the doctor, darling. Urgently."

"Poor thing. Another surgery, remember how difficult it was for her as a child."

"I do remember, but she was a child then, she's an adult now. A beautiful, strong, and hard-headed young woman."

"You're so proud of her."

"I am. You are too."

"I just love her with all my heart."

Alba turned and told them, "Thank you for being here for me."

"Of course," her mother said approaching the bed.

"Now, as the doctor said that it was urgent, shall we contact the Hölfang Foundation and explain the need to replace the BCI?"

"Yes, I guess the sooner the better, Dr. Tatsuo said 'urgently'."

"That's right, sweetheart, so we'll contact the Foundation to do the arrangements and prepare everything to travel back home as soon as possible. Now, you promised you'll eat at least some soup today, remember?"

"I will, Mom, but I'll rest a bit more before, my head hurts."

As she closed her eyes, Alba though of Dr. P. again.

I miss him so much. If I concentrate, I can see his face and almost hear his voice. The saddest part is that I still care for him, and I don't know how he is, I know nothing about him. We don't have any common friends and I don't know anybody in his family. It's as if he had died, yet he hasn't. He just doesn't want me. He didn't even reach out to check how I'm doing after the seizure. Who is that man? How can I still love him?

How could he? How could he leave me and disappear when I needed him most? What happened with all the plans he made for us? Was it all a lie? Was I just a toy that he grew bored of? Maybe he was always a terrible person and I never realized it. Was I so bad to him that I didn't deserve a proper goodbye? How could I fall for his lies? How could I ever believe that he was in love with me? Why did he leave me like that? Why did he run away from me?

Tired of the monologue in her head that repeated every day, Alba decided to put an end to it and just listen to the only possible answer.

Why? Because he never loved me.

DR. PATRICK FRÜHVETHSSON

Porto, January 16, 2034.

At the VIP area of the airport, Dr. Patrick Frühvethsson waited for a flight assistant to call him to board his plane sipping a whisky in front of the glass walls looking at planes and drones come and go.

This is it. My 'Porto" adventure is over. Back to the Maldives again.

Bored of looking outside, he checked the time again and then sat in a lounge chair. There, he thought about the sequence of events that had occurred last month.

It all started with a phone call...

*

Porto, four weeks before New Year's Eve.

"Mateen Fischer is on the line for you, Dr. P."

"Who?" He asked annoyed, with his coat on one arm and his laptop in the other.

"Mateen Fischer; he's a lawyer from Studer and Associates law firm."

"I don't know who that is. I'm on my way out; he can call again tomorrow."

"Apologies Dr. P. He says it's urgent."

Reluctantly, he took the call.

"Mr. Frühvethsson? Mr. Patrick Frühvethsson?"

"Yes, this is Dr. Patrick Frühvethsson speaking."

"Mr. Mateen Fischer here, Dr. Frühvethsson. I work as a lawyer at the Swiss legal company Studer and Associates. I'm contacting you to notify you that your father passed away two days ago as a result of injuries sustained in a drone accident. My heartfelt sympathy on your loss sir."

"My father? I don't understand."

"Yes, sir. He left you his home in his will, a chalet in the Alps. I'd like to set up a meeting with you to explain the paperwork and processes that are required in cases like this."

Dr. P. dropped his coat and his laptop on the floor. He was confused. He didn't feel sorry for his father's passing and wondered if he should be. At the same time, he was pleasantly surprised but shocked with the news of the inheritance.

"Sir?"

"..."

"Sir?"

"Yes, I can hear you. Sorry, I needed a moment to assimilate the news. Thanks for the call, Mr. Fischer. I appreciate it. My assistant will reach out to you to set up the meeting. Have a good evening."

In shock, he drove home. He parked at the garage in his apartment building and had a long look at his motorcycle. He found himself thinking about the motorcycle to avoid his mixture of emotions. *There is a part that needs to be replaced soon. It won't be easy to find a spare part. There are so few left for this old model. I'll have to work hard to find it.*

As he walked into his penthouse in a high building in the residential district of Boavista, he poured a whisky and sat on a classic brown Chesterfield sofa to process the news about his father. Glass in hand, he touched his neck, that was stiff sincc he answered the unexpected phone call.

My father? Today was the first time that someone addressed me as my father's son.

He's dead.

I guess I should be sad for his passing, but I never even met him, so I can't be. I can't be sad for him. The lawyer said he died in a drone accident. He also mentioned an inheritance – why would he leave me anything? He never wanted me.

His neck hurt, so he put a pillow beneath it.

He never acknowledged me as his son. Retaliation against my mother I suspect. Their marriage ended when my mother cheated on him when she was pregnant with me. Even after the paternity tests proved he was my father, he never acknowledged me. He never reached out, not even when my mother and my stepfather died three years ago in a car accident.

I hoped he'd reach out to me, I always did. I pursued a career in the same field and even the same places that he worked in expecting him to notice me. I hate to admit it but it's true. I admired him professionally. But I never wanted to carry his family name, at least I did that. And he never reached out.

The attorney said that I am to inherit a Swiss chalet. It makes no sense. Well... I've never been to the Alps...

*

Geneva, three weeks before New Year's Eve.

The moment he stepped out of the car, he felt uneasy. *It feels as if I'm about to break in. The real estate agent said they can't dispose of his things from the house unless I visit it. After the visit, I can sign off on the inventory they'll prepare. Then, everything can go, I don't want to keep anything. Then the house can be listed for sale. I just need to go in, look around and leave. Thirty minutes max.*

In front of the main door, he quickly looked at the house exterior with slate gable roof, large windows, traditional larches of wood cladding, and wide eaves.

As he entered, the first thing he noted was a large portrait of his father over a fireplace in a hunting outfit and several wall-mounted heads of roe deer. *I didn't know he was a hunter. Did he hunt those, or did he buy them along with the wooden furniture? I don't like being here. I'll just get this over with.*

He moved fast on the ground floor opening every drawer and cabinet he found. *Kitchen, walk-in pantry, and living room done. Upstairs now. A bedroom with en suite bathroom on one side and an office on the other, not much furniture again, it won't take long. Bedroom first.*

Seeing his father's clothes and personal belongings in the closet, dresser, and bathroom furnishing, he felt very uneasy again. *Now I really look like an intruder or a thief. Bedroom done, office now.*

At the office, he opened and closed the drawers of an old metal filing cabinet located under a two-by-two-meter mosaic replica of the Da Vinci Vitruvian man. Then he moved on to check the office desk.

He noticed a large cardboard box with a capital letter 'M' handwritten on it.

Wait, 'M' as in 'Alba's M?'

He placed the box on the desk.

What's inside the box?

Opening the lid, he found handwritten notebooks, paper documents, engineering drawings and printed photos. *Are these hand sketches? And notebooks... Who keeps paper records of their work?*

He checked the time, and then carried the box downstairs and placed it on a large coffee table.

Looking at his father's portrait he said out loud, "Well, Dr. Östmann, I suppose there was a reason why you kept this box here."

Ready to find answers, he emptied the contents of the box onto the coffee table, sat on a sofa, switched on a modern black curved reading lamp, put on his reading glasses, and browsed through the drawings and notebooks.

He studied M's engineering design sketches. *Nothing interesting here... Wait, is this M's serial number? It's different than the one in the Foundation's archives. I might be able to find M now. Alba will be thrilled if I manage to.* Then he read a report entitled 'Goals of the eMotional-Machine Program (eM-M-p)' and his father's notes about the principle of 'mimicry'. Putting the papers down, he reflected. *I have to give it to him – he was a visionary. Teaching human emotions to machines is still considered the holy grail in the field. And the idea of machine learning through mimicry from a single data source was very advanced back then. And the tear device? That was brilliant. But I've read all of these in the Foundation archives already.*

He stood up to stretch his back and went to the kitchen for a glass of water. Peering through the wide window above the sink, he saw tall and old pine trees. *What would Dr. Östmann say if he saw me here?* Then his mind shifted to Alba, to her smile, hair, and eyes. *She'll be so thrilled If I can find M for her.*

Back to the sofa, he picked two old, worn-out manila folders from the stack of contents. Intrigued by their titles, 'Symbiosis 1.0-external' and 'Symbiosis 1.0-internal', he leaned to read them.

A while later, he put all the contents back inside the box, closed the lid, grabbed his coat, and went outside. He walked fast for ten minutes down a gravel path and then stopped.

How could he? That man was insane! I need to calm down. Calm down and think. He took human tissue from Alba and wrapped it in an AI prototype. From Alba! Did he ask permission from her parents? I don't think so; Alba would know about it. So, he did it without consent! Did he expect it to grow? Outside a lab? There's no way it would grow! Of course, it didn't grow. Even today, tissue engineering is not advanced enough for that to happen. What was he thinking? Didn't he realize it was illegal? Even if the Foundations' board approved such an experiment, it was illegal. Why are there no records about any of this at the Foundation? Clearly because it was illegal.

Feeling the crisp air on his face and hands, he entered back into the house and paced in the living room looking at the box.

He was out of his mind. He invaded Alba's brain without consent. He used untested and aggressive technology on a child. The BCI he inserted has been sending electrical impulses into her brain for decades. He wanted to keep the serotonin level stable to avoid a potential mental depression, and he figured that sending an electrical current onto the pineal gland was the solution. That is an aggressive form of neurostimulation therapy that has failed all types of tests. And it's illegal.

I went through the records about Alba's bionic leg and the BCI that are available at the Foundation's archives, and everything seemed to be in order. There was no mention of any of this. Not even about the insertion of a piece of M's original design in the bionic leg to cheat the AI prototype into believing that part of it lived in Alba. I saw the engineering drawings and the technical specifications, and everything looked fine. There was nothing there to suggest any of this craziness.

How did he keep the board in the dark about the 'special feature' in the BCI as he called it? How did it bypass the Foundation's controls? Did he bribe the entire team working on the technology? I heard about corruption at the Foundation, but I assumed it was limited to the grants administration office. How much money did he spend on bribes?

Alba was only eight years old when he manipulated her brain. At that time her brain was still growing. He could have caused irreversible damage to it. This could have killed her. What side effects did it have?

He sat on the sofa and looked at the fireplace.

What should I do?

I need to think.

So, I found very unsettling facts about my biological father. The information relates to my employer and the woman I am involved with. In what ways does this affect me? Have I done anything wrong? No. Am I accountable for any wrongdoing? No, I'm not. So, what to do? I need to be practical. Alba still has the BCI. When I tell her about it, she'll rightfully sue Hölfang Industries. The company will find out we have a relationship and that she learned about the BCI from me. There'll be a scandal, and my name will be exposed. I'll get fired, and I won't get another job in the industry. I'll be the end of my career.

That can't happen.

That won't happen.

He stood up, took a photo of M's serial number from one of the papers and lit a fire. Then, he took the contents of the file box and put them one by one into the fire, watching them all burn. The manila folders, the engineering drawings, the notebooks, the paper photos, even the box, all went to the fire. When everything was reduced to ashes, he locked the house, put the keycard inside the mail box, and left.

*

Porto, two weeks before New Year's Eve.

"Good morning Dr. Waung."

"Dr. P., welcome, welcome. I waited for you, welcome."

Dr. P. observed the director of the data center. *Does he always wear a bowtie?* Then, he looked at the yellow color on the flooring, walls, and ceiling of at the data center, but didn't' say anything.

"I appreciate you making the time, Dr. Waung."

"Pleasure, pleasure Dr. P. Funny. Dr. P. Funny name."

"You promised to explain to me how the center works."

"Yes, Dr. P. I will explain it to you. The center is like a beehive. Very yellow," he added giggling. "Machine workers are 'worker bees'."

"What do the machine workers do?"

"Gather data, always gather data."

"Yes, but I mean, what do the machine workers do in relation to the beehive?"

"Caring for the 'queen' and 'larvae'."

"Who is the queen?"

"The queen is the Foundation."

"And the larvae?"

"The larvae are the units at the operations branch – Biomedical xLab, Maintenance unit, Genome xLab, Biomechatronics xLab..."

"Yes, the units."

"Yes, you know. The machine workers look for flowers."

"Flowers?"

"Flowers, data sources."

"And then?"

"The machine workers gather nectar. Nectar equals data."

"And?"

"Machine workers produce honey, information. Honey for the larvae."

Is he really a statistician? How long is he been working here? He looks ancient. I have to hand it to him, though, the organization of the workflow is impressive. But there is no excuse for the yellow color, beehive inspiration or not.

"That's such an impressive analogy, did you design the center?"

"Yes. A long time ago. I'm one of the oldest employees at the Foundation. I'm very proud. Data is very important, always."

"What are the workers bees working on today?"

"Today – various projects. Everyday projects."

"What projects?"

"Data gathering always."

"On what?"

"Today amphibious skin. For the Biomedical xLab to fabricate breathing devices, for underwater."

"Underwater breathing devices?"

"Yes, to breathe. Underwater."

"What data sources do the machine workers extract information from?"

"Any, any. Bee workers find any. And collect, categorize, analyze data. Non-stop. They are always working."

"So, they are programmed to find data sources?"

"Yes, the bee workers are like data detectives. Looking for flowers always. Always."

"Flowers."

"Bee workers find data sources. If they are open, they are easy to access. If they are not open, the Foundation makes a data sharing agreement with the owner and opens it that way."

"I see."

"There are many, many agreements. Tens of thousands. The data center is very old. I'm also very old," he added giggling again. "We have agreements with public centers. Companies also. Worldwide."

"Tell me more about the type of data machine workers access?"

"Any. Any type. Texts, videos, life experiments, sensors. They are programmed to look for data always, like the bison."

"The bison?"

"Yes, the bison never stops eating. Even when they are walking, they are always eating."

"Bison? I didn't know that. What about the quality of the data sources? How is the validity of the data sources checked? Who verifies the metadata?"

"The machine workers do."

"How?"

"Like the spider."

"Like the spider?"

"Yes, like the spider."

"You'll tell me all about spiders next time Dr. Waung. I don't want to take more of your time, you've been too generous." Dr. P. said checking the time. "You said when I called that you had located the machine worker with the serial number I sent you, right? Could I quickly see it?"

"Yes, yes, I do this. For you. This way."

Dr. Waung guided Dr. P through rooms and corridors in the data center.

"Third in the row. One, two, three. Three" he said pointing at a machine worker. "It is tracking sea turtles now in the Caribbean Sea."

So that's M...

"Dr. Waung, it was good to see you. I look forward to learning more about your animal analogies."

"Yes, yes. Don't be a stranger Dr. P."

*

Rio, New Year's Eve.

"You can wait there, sir," a medical admin at the São José hospital told him. "As soon as the doctors have an update about your friend, we'll let you know."

Update? The only update I want to hear is that Alba is all right. The doctor said she's in a coma. She was fine the whole day. What happened? Resting his head on both hands, he looked at the floor for a while. Then stood up and paced up and down.

The seizure must be related to the special feature that my... that Dr. Östmann... put into the BCI. I should have told her. But after my trip to the Alps, I scrutinized Alba's records of her quarterly check-ups and I found no red flags anywhere. No evidence of the BCI malfunctioning and no sign of irregular brain activity. My assumption was the only possible one – if Alba hadn't had any side effects from the electric currents sent towards her pineal gland yet, she was unlikely to have them in the future.

He sat down, looking at the medical assistant who worked behind a screen.

To be on the safe side, I was going to advise her to replace the BCI. I was going to say that with a new generation model, the communication with the bionic leg would be even better.

But I didn't want to do it during our holiday, I was going to do it afterwards.

I should have told her about my trip to the Alps.

How can I face her now? What will she think of me?

What do I do now?

He checked the time once more.

If I tell her now about the BCI my career will be over.

I can't lose my job. Even if that means losing her.

I do like her a lot, but it wasn't going to last anyway. We want different things. She wants me to meet her friends and family and wants to meet mine. She wants us to do the things that couples do. To be a couple. And I don't. I never wanted that. All I wanted was to have her.

I was already thinking of accepting the offer to go back to my job in the Maldives, I don't like Porto much.

I must go on with my life.

And standing up, he left.

M

Porto, February 01, 2033.

M was scanning the Australian Phasmatodea Encyclopedia of Insects that dated from a century earlier, when one of its sensors connected automatically to a device via Bluetooth. The machine worker paused, scanning a double page dedicated to the Lamprima Aurata. The device it connected to was equipped with a class-one micro radio Bluetooth and was located one hundred and sixty-three meters away.

Programmed as an effective bee worker at the Beehive, to collect data non-stop from any available data source, M identified the device as a new 'flower' and then launched a series of commands to collect all available data on it, the 'nectar'.

It created a database and entered the geographical coordinates of the location: Latitude: 41° 14' 14.76" N and

Longitude: - 8° 61' 14.80." Overlaying a cartographic map of Porto, it recorded additional data: stop 32 of the 500-bus. And added the time stamp: 8:52 AM and date: February 01, 2033.

Then, it continued working.

Finishing the Australian Phasmatodea Encyclopedia of Insects, M approached a pile of old books and took another insect's encyclopedia for scanning. The process was slow because the books were old and delicate.

At the same time, it continued tracking the connected device. To record its location with more detail, it overlayed a map of the Foundation's premises. From 08:55 to 10:26, the device moved from the main entrance of the Foundation to the HR unit, from there to the operations branch and then to the Instituto de Pensamento. At 13:32 the device left the premises and went to the Italian restaurant Pizzeria Baixa, then back to the Instituto de Pensamento, and at 18:09 left again on Mouzinho da Silveira street. At this point the device was out of range and M could not record more locations.

Then, it cross-referenced the movements and routes of the device with the activity of the Foundation's employees' chips and deducted that the device was linked to an employee whose first name was Alba.

TOGETHER

Porto, March 17, 2034.

In bed, Alba drifted away. Feeling the chilly night air on her face, she heard her feet tapping the beach boardwalk. The sky was dark, with only a thin crescent moon visible, no stars. Her arms felt the wind beneath them. Her body felt light and balanced softly, as if carried forward by a current. She surrendered to it as if floating on the current was a natural thing to do.

The air current took her to a forest, and she was shocked to find it was broad daylight. There were oak trees covered with English ivy on them. She felt the soil, wet. Looking down, she realized she wasn't wearing shoes and saw tree bark, brown leaves, and lichen-coated branches beneath her bare feet. Resting on a large, round granite stone, she touched tiny succulent plants and moss. A gentle breeze blew her hair. As she rearranged it, a small brown bird feather fell from her hair. She couldn't see anybody around but had the impression that she wasn't alone. She liked it there – it was peaceful.

Following a path, she walked down an aisle of tree branches and bracken and saw butterfly wings. Some were small, purple, blue, and yellow; others were large and transparent, with thin silver threads on them. At the end of the path, she came across a meadow. The light was almost white there and very bright. Dark pink flowers shone on a carpet of green grass.

Taking in their beauty, she bent down to pick one. Then, the ground trembled. Softly at first, and then violently, until it shook beneath her feet.

She panicked, lost her balance, and fell.

She opened her eyes and looked around. It was dark. Seeing the emergency lights in the room, she realized she was at the Foundation hospital.

What was that? It felt so real. So real. It must have been a vivid dream. I haven't had one of those in a really long time. I'm thirsty. I need water. It was real – the trees, the feather, the trembling ground – all of it. It wasn't scary, it was so peaceful, until the shaking of the ground. Was it a dream? I felt I was awake. I used to have experiences like that as a child. I'd go to strange places, then get lost, go through loopholes... Mom and Dad got worried. The pediatrician said they were 'vivid dreams'.

She had some water and checked the time.

I better go back to sleep again, it is the middle of the night.

*

She changed her position in the hospital bed again. *What is the time? Is it afternoon already? I'm so tired of being here. How long is it since the surgery? A month? Two? I lose track of time. I like this room more than the one I was in after the BCI replacement at the Foundation's branch in Gaia. How long have I been in this room? A week already? At least this room is nice. It doesn't look like a hospital room. It looks like a guest room in a Portuguese country home. It's much nicer than the one in Rio, that was really bad.* Then it hit her, again – she remembered the moment she woke up in São José Hospital and Dr. P. wasn't by her side. *How could he? How could he? Dad says I've got to stop asking the question and just move on with my life, but I just can't. Until today, no news from him, nothing. And I guess he knows nothing about me, or my life and he doesn't care. M disappeared. Patrick left. And since the seizure I feel there is someone else missing from my life, but I can't remember who.*

Uncomfortable, she turned again. *Who brought those flowers? It might have been Mom or Aunt Albertina. They are so sweet, coming here to see me every day. Also, Dad is here when he can make it. They say I'm like a zombie. I'm glad because the surgery to replace the BCI went well but I guess I don't look glad to them. And I'm having bizarre experiences lately. I fear that I'm going completely nuts.*

As she moved again trying to find a comfortable position in bed, she heard a familiar sound. It was a 'vuuptz, vuuptz' sound.

She knew that sound well. Though decades had passed, she could recognize it among a million sounds.

What? Am I awake? I hope I'm awake.

She turned.

"M?"

*

"M? M! It's you. Is it you?"

She observed a machine worker that looked like M and stood still and quiet in the middle of the room. *It looks like M, but it might be another machine worker that just looks like it.*

"Do you know who I am?"

"Yes."

"Who am I?"

"Subject_Alba."

Any machine worker could find that information in the eM-M-p files in the Foundation's archives.

"What was my favorite stuffed animal when I was a child?"

"A dolphin."

Was that on the files also?

"What is my favorite ice-cream topping?"

"Sprinkles."

That might also be in the files. I don't know what to ask that wouldn't be.

"M, move to the room's entrance and back," she said.

As the machine did this, listening to the familiar sound, Alba's eyes filled with tears of joy. *It is M. It is M. No other machine worker sounds the same way.*

She looked at her old companion for a while.

"M, it's you, it's really you." She had a million questions to ask. "How did you find me?"

"41°.14'19.23" Latitude, -8°.61'63.05" Longitude."

"What?"

"41°.14'19.23" Latitude, -8°.61'63.05" Longitude."

"Those are geographical coordinates. What are you? a compass now?" she said bursting into laughter.

"No."

"So, how did you find me?"

"41°.14'19.23" Latitude, -8°.61'63.05" Longitude, room number 36, Hospital de São Francisco do Porto. Health facility."

"Yes, I know I'm at the hospital M, I wasn't asking you where I am. How... Okay let me try something else, why are you here now M?"

"The visit to the health facility in this location lasts and average of fifty minutes. Your latest visit has been for seven days. Seven days is an anomaly. There is high probability of a health problem. I told Dr. Waung that there is an anomaly, that there is a high probability of a health problem, maybe my assistance is needed," M said. Then, pointing at Alba's bionic leg it added, "This is me."

"What?"

"This is me."

M has gone nuts.

"I didn't get a word of what you just said. Do you know Dr. P.? I mean Dr. Frühvethsson?"

"The former director of the Biomechatronics xLab."

"Did you ever meet him?"

"I had visual contact of him when he visited the Beehive. December 17, 2033."

Before travelling to Rio for New Year's Eve. He told me he found M before travelling to Rio. At least he didn't lie about that. Is M here because of him?

"Your visit today, has it anything to do with Dr. Frühvethsson?"

"Your question is not clear to me."

"Did you find me here today because Dr. Frühvethsson visited the Beehive?"

"No."

Then, how come you are here?

"So, you being here is about geographical coordinates? I don't understand anything. You'll have to explain that again later. But first I need to know what happened to you. You left home, my home in the middle of the night, why? I was a kid when you left, and I couldn't even say goodbye to you, and I really missed you afterwards, a lot. You were gone overnight, and I never knew why. Why did you leave?"

"I malfunctioned."

"What do you mean 'malfunctioned'?"

"I crashed."

Crashed? I never thought about that possibility.

"Did you? What happened? How did it happen?"

"Too complex."

"What was too complex."

"You."

"Me? What are you talking about?"

"I crashed because of you. Too complex."

I understand less and less. Was M always so difficult to understand?

"And what happened then, after you crashed?"

"I was relocated. To the Logistics unit."

"And after that?"

"I was relocated to the Genome xLab, then the Biomechanical xLab, then the Beehive."

The Beehive.

"So, you've been working at the Foundation all these years."

"Your question is not clear to me."

"Have you been working at the Foundation since you left my home?"

"Yes."

So, every quarter, when I came to do my quarterly check at this hospital, year after year, M was just a few meters away.

"How long have you been working at the Beehive?"

"One year, three months and five days."

So just before I started working at the Instituto de Pensamento.

"Come, come closer to me, I want to see you closer, don't just stand there. You're shorter than I remember you."

M approached the bed.

"Look at you! You look fantastic! So many new pieces! You've been upgraded quite a bit!"

"Upgrades are conducted on a bimonthly basis, software and mechanical pieces."

"Well, old friend, upgraded or not you haven't changed the way you talk," she said bursting into laughter again.

"Now, I want to hear everything about you since the beginning. Or better not, listen to me first, I'll tell you everything first. After you left..."

*

Alba suddenly realized that there was someone standing in the doorway, watching her and M.

Who is this now?

"Good afternoon," she said.

"Good afternoon. Pleasure, pleasure, Dr. Alba."

"You are?"

"Sorry, sorry, so rude. Dr. Waung, director of the Beehive."

"Dr. Waung, an honor to meet you, sir. Are you here for M?"

"Intriguing, most intriguing," he said looking at M. "May I come in Dr. Alba?"

"Of course, please do come in."

What is going on here? I don't understand anything. He seems nice.

"Dr. Alba. Junior researcher at Instituto de Pensamento. Very good. Very talented," he said entering the room.

How does he know where I work? Because he read my HR file, of course, life at the Foundation. Why did he read my HR file?

"May I sit?"

"Of course, Dr. Waung."

"How is your health? You are feeling good for a little chat with Dr. Waung?"

"Yes, sure," she said, arranging the pillows in the bed and sitting straight.

What on Earth is going on? Why are M and Dr. Waung in my room? I was so excited to see M that didn't realised how odd is that it just showed up out of the blue.

"Very intriguing, Dr. Alba."

"Excuse me?"

"I will explain. The machine worker said, 'health problem'. 'Health problem' and gave geographical coordinates."

"It told me the same, what's the meaning of it?" she said, looking at M who remained quiet by her side.

"Machine workers are programmed to monitor their own systems. They detect if there is a need of maintenance. They give alerts. I asked, 'Is maintenance needed?'. The answer was the same – 'health problem' and geographical coordinates.

"So, you are saying that M told you that there was a health problem and then gave you the coordinates to my room? How is it possible? I haven't seen M since I was a child, how could M know I was here?"

"Very intriguing. You know this machine worker, Dr. Alba."

"Yes, I participated in one of the Foundation's programs when I was a child. The eMotional-Machine program, the eM-M-p. M lived with me and my family for over two years."

"Yes, very nice. I saw that in your HR file."

He looked at M for a long while. After a few minutes, he spoke again.

"Now, mystery-solving time."

"Why are you here?" he asked M.

"The visit to the health facility in this location lasts and average of fifty minutes. The latest visit was seven days. Seven days is an anomaly. There was a high probability of health problem. Maybe my assistance was needed," M said. Then, pointing at Alba's bionic leg added, "This is me."

Alba looked at Dr. Waung astonished, "Why is it saying, 'seven days is an anomaly'? I think I've been in this room for a week now. And why is it saying, 'this is me'?"

"I don't know," Dr Waung answered, also looking astonished.

"May I ask you to move your bedsheet? So sorry, so inconvenient," he said.

"It's not a problem," she said, uncovering her leg.

"Thank you, thank you Dr. Alba. So sorry. May I approach?"

"Sure."

Then, Dr. Waung asked again.

Pointing at her bionic leg, M answered the same way as before. "This is me."

Alba looked at the scientist, perplexed.

"Intriguing, most intriguing," he said.

What is going on here?

"M, this leg is mine, not yours. What is 'you'?"

M approached the leg and touched a small black piece.

"This is me."

Alba was speechless.

"How did you find that piece?" Dr. Waung asked.

"Tracking."

"Tracking that piece? Why?"

"Flower. Track it to obtain nectar."

"Very, very outstanding," Dr. Waung said.

A flower? Nectar?

"You discovered this flower, when?"

"February 01, 2033."

"That's the day I started working at the Instituto de Pensamento."

"Outstanding."

"How do you track it?" he asked.

"Class-one micro radio Bluetooth."

Dr. Waung remained quiet for a few minutes, looking at M. Finally, he got up and said: "Dr. Alba, you rest. Now. I will analyse this situation, and we will talk more later."

"Thank you, Dr. Waung."

Is M also leaving? I don't want M to leave.

"Mr Waung, this might sound like a strange request to you, but could M be temporarily deployed at the hospital to stay with me? M helped me to recover from my leg amputation as a child. As you see, I'm recovering again. M could help me to cheer up a bit, and believe me, I need that. I've seen some machine workers around here."

Dr. Waung looked at her tenderly.

"I see. I will speak with Dr. Luana. Hospital director."

"Thank you, I'm really grateful for that."

"You rest now. Please you rest."

"Thank you. By sir. Bye for now M."

*

As soon as her old friend and the director of the Beehive left, Alba called her mom. "Mom, Mom, you won't believe what just happened."

"Sweetheart? Is there something wrong? Do you need anything?"

"No, Mom, all is good. You are not going to believe it. I was just with M. Like M, M. It found me! It was just here with me in the room, at the hospital."

"M? What do you mean it found you? After all these years? Are you sure it was M?"

"I'll tell you more later when you come. I just wanted to tell you that I'm so happy. I feel that things are going to change for me now. And I know now that you didn't hide anything from me when M left. It malfunctioned, Mom, that's why it was taken away."

"Malfunctioned? What was it doing? It was in the middle of the night."

"It crashed, apparently. I don't know why."

"Crashed... Unbelievable. What do you mean about 'hiding things from you? Of course, we didn't hide anything.'"

"I mean about M's disappearance and where it was. I know now you didn't know. I'm so sorry I thought you did."

"But sweetheart, we told you many times..."

"I know, Mom, I know. I'm sorry but I always thought you didn't tell me the truth. But now I know you did. I love you and I'm so grateful to you and Dad for coming to Rio and being by my side and taking such good care of me always. Please also tell Dad."

"Of course, sweetheart, we love you with all our heart. I'm sorry to hear you held this worry inside for so long."

"Me too, Mom, me too."

"What happens now? Are you going to see M again?"

*

Porto, March 19, 2034.

"Here is the transcript," Dr. Waung said showing her a large digital portable screen.

Alba was looking forward to hearing what the director of the Beehive had discovered from M, who was behaving quite strangely, and also the answer to her request about having M stay with her.

"This is a briefing from Dr. Östmann dated May 02, 2013, for the Foundation's board. I will read it for you. "Following the amputation of her left leg, subject_A had a bionic prosthesis attached. The prosthesis was developed by the Engineering Lab and includes a piece that was taken from machine_M. Machine_M is connected to the piece through a micro-Bluetooth embedded in it and 'believes' that its part of its own system. Why did I do this? I did it to trick machine_M into believing a part of itself 'lives' in subject_A. Why? As per the Foundation's protocols, all AI prototypes are designed to be responsible for monitoring that their systems are up to date, with the support of the Maintenance unit of course. Making Machine_M believe that a piece of its systems lives in subject_A will create a bond with subject_A."

Alba was speechless. She looked at M, at the bionic leg, and back at M.

"Wow."

"A highly unusual experiment. Good. Smart."

"But why did M track me? Was it programmed for it?"

"Because M is looking for data, always. Flowers."

"Flowers?"

"At the Beehive, flowers are data sources. Machine workers are bee workers. They are programmed to find data sources, flowers."

Is he saying I'm a flower for M now?

"So, you are saying that when M was deployed at the Beehive, it was programmed to look for new data sources constantly."

"Yes."

"So, when I started working at the Foundation last year, M connected via Bluetooth with this piece and then tracked its location. As I've been hospitalized for over a week, M concluded that the piece needed maintenance because of a 'health problem'."

"Yes."

"Wow."

"Now, you rest. M can stay."

"Did you speak with Dr. Luana and she agrees to let M stay with me here?"

"Dr. Luana says yes. I say yes also," he answered, giggling.

"Oh, thank you, thank you Dr. Waung."

"I have a little request. What if M helps you and we study your relationship? You and the machine worker, very nice together. Two colleagues come here every day to study, to observe, not to interfere. For a few hours."

"So, you will send two colleagues to observe M and me for a few hours every day here, and M can stay with me during my recovery."

"Yes. That's my idea."

"I agree, it'd be wonderful if M can stay."

"I'm very impressed. You and the machine worker together are very nice."

"Thank you so much."

"No, no, no. No need. Now, you rest, please, you rest. Later."

I can't believe it. It's the best news ever. M is going to be here with me. I don't mind being observed. I like being part of a study that Dr. Waung is directing – he is a legend.

*

After Dr. Waung left, Alba chatted with M.

"So, M, you said you crashed the night you left. What on Earth were you doing to crash my old friend?"

"Too complex."

"Yes, I know, you said that already. I won't leave this bed for weeks. Lay and rest, that's all I've got to do. I have all the time in the world, so go on, start talking. Tell me everything."

"…"

Okay, I remember, clear instructions or questions to you…

"M, what were you doing the night you crashed and left?"

"Building a model for aesthetic appreciation."

"You mean like a model to reproduce the emotion aesthetic appreciation? Cool!"

"Yes. To build the model…"

"Wait, wait, was that your first model for an emotion?"

"No."

"So, which one did you build before?"

"Joy. I built a model for joy successfully."

"So cool. Go on."

"To build the model, I looked for patterns on how you expressed the emotion."

"Tell me about my patterns."

"There is a pattern in the trigger. Aesthetic appreciation is triggered in subject_A by…"

"Who's subject_A?"

"You."

"I know, I'm teasing you. Go on."

"Aesthetic appreciation is triggered in subject_A by an external stimulus. The catalyst is an element from nature, either a single one, such as a flower, or a group forming a scene, such as a sunset over a water surface. After noticing the element or elements through observation, subject_A focuses on it, or them. Stops speaking or playing abruptly and zooms in visually into the stimulus, focusing on it from one to three minutes. In such instances, if someone calls or throws a ball at subject_A, she doesn't respond."

"Wait, can you stop calling me subject_A?"

"Subject_A is used in the notes."

"Oh, you're reading the notes you made that night so it's subject_A for me then."

"Yes."

"Fine, go on."

"There is a pattern in the facial expression. It changes from wonder to relaxation and then serenity."

"Really?"

"Yes."

"Go on."

"There is a pattern in the body. After contemplating the stimulus, subject_A takes deep breaths (one to four), zooms out her vision, and tilts her head slightly to the left and up. Afterwards, she stares at the horizon, even if there is a wall in front of her, and then closes her eyes. After that, she looks at the stimulus again. The heartbeat decreases linearly at that point."

Alba was fascinated with the description of herself experiencing an emotion as a child.

"You're fascinating M, go on."

"There are common characteristics in the speech. After further contemplating the stimulus, subject_A compliments its beauty with verbal expressions. The most common phrases are 'look, this is so beautiful' and 'oh, look, have you ever seen anything this beautiful?' Subject_A speaks more slowly, with long, muted pauses between word tokens, spending longer time on each utterance, in both vocal and non-vocal sounds, and introducing more pauses. The volume and the pitch used are below average."

"No pattern in the speech characteristics? Only 'common characteristics'?"

"Yes. I found anomalies in the speech characteristics."

"Wait, I'm getting lost. You said you 'crashed' building a model for aesthetic appreciation, correct?"

"Yes."

"When did you crashed?"

"Doing analysis."

"Analysis of what?"

"Of the anomalies."

"Okay, okay, back to the anomalies then. What anomalies did you find in my speech?"

"Musical timbre of the voice and refined choice of words that correspond to an adult, not a child's vocabulary."

"Okay... What did you do then?"

"I searched to find data sequences with the same anomalies."

"And?"

"I found forty-two."

"Forty-two what?"

"I found forty-two data sequences. All had the label: 'for further analysis'.

"What did you do then?"

"I re-calculated all measurements and formulas in the forty-two data sequences."

"What happened then?"

"I found another anomaly: an abnormal level of glow in subject_A's eyes."

Alba was enjoying the chat with M but starting to wonder what the meaning of the 'anomalies' found by M was.

"And then?"

"I built a complex artificial neural network to find relationships, connections, and associations among all the data points in the forty-two sequences."

"And?"

"I crashed. Too complex."

Alba was now very curious about the anomalies.

"The fact that you crashed is clear. But can you be a bit more descriptive to explain to me the issue about the anomalies?"

"Your question is not clear to me."

"M, examples, give me examples of the forty-two data sequences."

"I show."

"Can you show me? Movies of myself as a child? Yes! Show me!"

Pressing a button, M projected a movie in the room.

Alba saw herself in her school uniform, walking home and talking to M. She laughed, hearing how fast she talked and how much she gestured with her hands.

I look so cheerful.

In the movie, she was telling M a story about something that happened to her at lunchtime. Then, she stopped walking and talking abruptly and stared at a man who was seated on a bench. She gazed at the horizon for a brief moment and then said, "I am so sorry for his family – it will be a challenge for them."

"What will be a challenge?" M asked.

"Seeing him go. He will be leaving soon, probably before Christmas."

"Where do you think he is going?"

"He will go up. And from there onwards, as it happens when we die."

"Life expectancy at birth for men in Portugal is 78 years. The gentleman looks like he is in his late sixties, probably he will live longer."

"People have colors M. I see them. His color tells me that he will be leaving soon."

The movie ended here.

Alba remained quiet. She didn't know what to make out of what she just saw.

"Show me another one."

M showed her another movie in which she was playing with a ball at the Parque Cidade, the large park close to Porto. Then she stopped kicking the ball all of a sudden and walked towards a tree. After caressing the trunk, she touched some of the leaves in the low branches gently. Then looked past the tree for a moment and said, "I hear you, dear one. I understand. I will, I promise, and I thank you." After bowing slightly and then stroking the trunk again, she dashed to continue playing with the ball.

As the second new movie ended, Alba still remained quiet.

"Another one," she said.

In the next movie, she saw herself playing on a beach. She was jumping over the waves on the shore and, as in the previous one, stopped suddenly. Then, she picked up a small, white, surf-tumbled quartz pebble, examined it, gazed at the ocean, and told M, "I will find more like this one. I will put them next to the bed to accompany me at night when I journey. Don't you find them beautiful? See the crystals in them."

"At night in bed, you do not travel, you sleep."

"Of course, I do, though most of the time I do not remember where I go, that is certain."

The third movie ended there.

*

"Did I say, 'I journey at night?' That makes total sense. M, I've been having the strangest experiences since the surgery, and every time I felt as if I was journeying somewhere. The sequence is always the same: I'm running at the beach, then I'm in a forest, then down a path and into a meadow. It's all very surreal. I used to have the same experiences as a child and the doctors called it 'vivid dreams' but I don't think they are dreams – I think they are something else. What do you think?"

"Your question is not clear to me."

When M said this, Alba had a revelation. She just realized the reason why she bonded with M as a child.

I thought my bond with M was because of the time we spent together and because it took care of me specially after the surgery. Also, because I felt special for being selected to be in the eM-M-p and because M helped me feel better about myself, M was cool, so I was also cool with the bionic leg.

But there was much more. Much.

I always told M everything. I told M that I travelled at night. I never told anyone else. As I didn't tell anyone about the strange experiences I've been having since the BCI was replaced. I haven't told my parents, or my closest friends. And I just told M right now. Why? Because I can say anything to M and M won't judge me. M accepts me as I am.

Because M can't distinguish what is labelled as 'normal' by society. As a kid I spoke to M freely, I behaved freely without fear of being labeled as 'crazy'. M was the only one with whom I could be myself. I spoke about people's auras, and I caressed trees in front of M.

But what happened to me? I only remember vaguely the things that are in the movies, my 'anomalies' as M labeled them. There is something about the experiences I'm having now related to all this, I feel it.

Alba asked M to show her the other movies with her 'anomalies'. After watching them all, she felt hopeful and knew that her saudades would soon end. She just knew.

Feeling gratitude for all she had in her life, looking at M she asked: "So M, do you like working at the Beehive?"

"I am not programmed to like."

"Yes, I do know that."

"What about this – do you prefer working with data or with people?"

"I'm not programmed to prefer."

"What's your purpose, M?"

"To complete my tasks."

Alba looked through the window for a moment, realizing how much he had to thank the black and shiny machine that kept on answering all her questions, regardless of their relevance or meaning.

"So, M, did you ever learn how to cry?"

"I did not."

"Would you like me to teach you?"

"Yes."

"Here we go then. Basically, there are three reasons to cry – you cry when you're very sad, when you're having physical pain or when you are very, very happy. Where do you want me to start?"

"From the beginning."

"Of course! The beginning it is. So, in order to cry..."

SEASHELL WITH GOLDEN TRACES

Porto, April 30, 2034.

Alba put on her gardening gloves, looked at the soil, tools, and jasmine plants lying on the terrace floor at her apartment and then looked at the flowerpots that were filled with weeds. *Gardening today. I'm going back to work tomorrow, and I want to finish the apartment re-decoration before that.*

She pulled the weeds, but they were firmly anchored in the soil and didn't move. As she pulled harder, a few came out, but most of the long, strong roots remained attached to large blocks of dry soil. Using a shovel, she emptied the flowerpots and threw their contents in a plastic bag. Then she refilled the flower pots with soil and planted the jasmine plants. Happy with the task accomplished, she prepared a tea and rested on a teak chair. *Oh, the sun, nice. It's so nice to not be in a hospital, resting at home is much better. First Rio and then Porto, weeks, and more weeks, that was way too much.*

She looked inside her apartment. *My work paid off. I do like the new pendant copper lamp. And the mellow coral tones in the walls. And the aquamarine-patterned rug and matching pillows, they are stunning. This place needed some color, it was too plain, as is my life.*

She glanced down at the plastic bag lying on the floor. *Finding weeds in a flower pot is like finding chunks of resentment in your heart. Even though you knew they were there, you are surprised at how much they have grown. Once you see them, you don't want them to stay. Weeds thrive in all types of soil, rich or poor in nutrients, and leave no room for anything else to grow. Just as resentment grows in the heart, leaving no room for anything else.*

*

Swiftly, Alba changed into her running gear, grabbed the plastic bag from the floor and left the apartment. After disposing of the garbage, she headed to the beach. She enjoyed the feeling of having strength in her body back again.

Then, she ran faster than she had since she was back home. And every stride brought back painful memories: when she awoke in a hospital alone and Dr. P. was nowhere to be found, when she waited for an answer to her email, and when he hung up on her. Trying to discard her thoughts, she ran until she was exhausted.

Catching her breath in front of the ocean, she thought about the weeds and decided it was time to let the painful memories go away and empty her heart of resentment. Staring at the white foam, she took off her shoes, put her earplugs and comms band inside, and walked towards the sea.

As her feet touched the cold water, she surrendered. Freezing but determined, she continued walking until the water reached her waist. *I need to move on with my life. I need room for new things. I can't hold inside what I don't need any longer.*

Submerging her body, she let the water wash away the emotions she no longer needed.

*

On the way back home, she was soaking wet but feeling very at ease about it.

Now I smell like mussels.

Unintentionally, she found herself at the iron gate of the Farol da Nostra Senhora Da Luz. As many times before, she read the plate on the outside wall. 'Built by charter from the Marques de Pombal, dated February 1st, 1758, due to difficulties in entering the Duoro River, which had long required the construction of a lighthouse. The chosen location was the privileged Monte da Luz, whose view extends from Barra do Douro to Espinho, and where the Chapel of Nossa Senhora da Luz, dating from the 17th century, once existed. In the granite outcrop, a set of rupestrian rock engravings were recently discovered. Municipal Chamber of the City of Porto.'

I've never seen the prehistoric art. Where will it be? Under the plants? Maybe it faded away with time.

As she searched for the engravings on the granite stones, covered with tiny succulent plants and moss, she remembered the moss, the path, and the trembling ground. Closing her eyes, she concentrated to make sense of the experience. But instead of the moss, she saw a white seashell with golden traces on it.

What?

She opened her eyes.

What?

She touched her forehead.

Am I ill? No, I don't think I am. I feel good; in fact, I feel really good. What was that?

Back home, she had a long shower, smiling when she found algae on her legs, and sat in the sun for a while.

Feeling the warmth of the sun she relaxed, when she closed her eyes, the white seashell with golden traces appeared in her mind again.

She marvelled at the image and paid attention to the details, getting lost in it. Then, she heard a song:

'Waves, waves, waves of blue,

coming and going in a dance with you.

Despair and joy, rage, and compassion,

crashing and going in a dance with you.

Waves, waves, waves of blue,

coming and going in a dance with you.

Grief and desire, hope, and bliss,

crashing and going in a dance with you.

Waves, waves, waves of blue,

coming and going in a dance with you.

Flooding and chaos in the order of things.

Tearing of time ...

in a wave...

with you.

Waves, waves, waves of blue...'

Opening her eyes, she jumped off the chair and called her mom.

"Mom?"

"Hi, sweetheart."

"Do you remember that as a kid, I used to have what the doctors called 'vivid dreams'? I think I'm having those experiences again; And I don't think they are dreams."

"Sweetheart, wait, we just had lunch at your aunt's, Albertina. Let me go to a quiet place so we can talk. All right, I'm in the garden now; tell me what happened. Dreams? What dreams?"

"Yes, I'm having what the doctors called 'vivid dreams' when I was a child. But I don't think they are dreams because I'm awake when I'm experiencing them. It's all very strange but not scary strange. I heard a song today. And I remember that I used to hear it every night as a child."

"A song?"

"Yes."

"You never told us about a song."

"I guess not. So, what do you think, Mom?"

"I think you've just recovered from surgery and a shock. Remember, you were in a coma. Are you anxious about going back to work tomorrow? Did you cry today again about the break-up with that man?"

"No, I'm not anxious, Mom, and I didn't cry today, I haven't cried in days in fact."

"Are you eating well?"

"Yes, Mom, I'm eating well. I guess I'm just tired."

"Yes, that might be it, you're just tired sweetheart."

"Are you sleeping enough? My dear, you need to rest. Remember what the doctors said – 'rest, rest, and rest'."

"You're right, Mom, I guess I could rest more. How was the lunch? What did Aunt Albertina make?"

"The lunch was very nice. Your aunt made bacalau a bras for us, her signature dish. It was delicious. We were having coffee now."

"Thank you, Mom, I let you go back to Dad and Aunt. Send my love to them. See you on Wednesday. I love you."

*

After a light lunch and some rest, Alba met her childhood friend, Leonela for a stroll by the riverside.

"Alba! Look at you! You look fantastic."

"Thank you, Leonela, you look good too. I love your sweater, is it cashmere? The color suits you, very pretty."

"Thanks, yes, it's cashmere. But you're shining! There's something different about you. What is it?"

"I don't know. I feel good, that's for sure."

"Did you go for a run today?"

"Yes, and I had a splash in the cold water."

"No, you didn't."

"Yes, I did. I'm a real local now."

The friends sat at a lounge terrace where a DJ played music.

"Tell me, dear, how are you doing?"

"I'm feeling good, rested, strong. Also, different, as if something has changed in me, but I don't know what it is."

"Again, you look great."

"Thank you. There's something I wanted to talk to you about."

"Tell me."

"I don't know how to explain it. Don't freak out. I'm going to tell you something that might sound weird."

"Weird?"

"As a child, I used to see colors on people, and I can see them again now. The same with smell. I could smell things that I didn't see and also see things but not with my eyes. And it's all coming back. Are you freaking out?"

"No, not really."

"No?"

"No, I'm not surprised. When we were kids, you were different."

"Was I?"

"Yes."

"What do you mean different?"

"It's difficult to explain. Different in a good way. You'd speak about things like life or death, as if you were an old professor giving a lecture. I thought you were funny when you spoke like that."

"I didn't know I was doing that."

"You did that a lot."

"Do you remember when we heard that girl from the sixth grade, Morgan, was taken to a psychiatric hospital?"

"Yes, of course, that was the highlight of the school's gossip for a long time."

"When I heard about that girl, I was so scared. I thought that if someone knew about my experiences, I'd be locked up forever."

"Oh, no! I'm so sorry. It must have been very scary for you."

"It was. I never spoke about my experiences with anyone, only with M."

"With M?"

"Yes, I guess I felt I could be myself with M, I didn't need to hide anything for fear of been locked up."

"Wow."

"When I grew up, I didn't have those experiences anymore and I even forgot I had them as a child. And now, since I had a seizure, it's all coming back."

"Since the seizure?"

"Yes, it's like it is all back since that night. At the beach, before I fainted, I saw something but not with my eyes; it was so real. Then something exploded in my head."

"Wow."

"Yes, it's all coming back."

"Are you scared?"

"No, not really. Curious."

"But if you had those experiences as a child and now recently again, what happened in between?"

"I have no idea. And I don't think it matters anyway. I feel peace inside now."

"And you say, you started to experience things again since the seizure?"

"It started the day of the seizure, then gradually. I today, after the splash in the ocean, I felt inside as I used to feel as a child, but I can't explain it with words."

"What about the splash made you feel different?"

"Well, I think it is because I finally let go of the resentment I had against Patrick."

"Well…"

"I know. But I needed to let go of the resentment. I have forgiven him."

"After what he did to you? After the months you spent crying because of the way he left and afterwards ghosted you? Sorry to say it that way, but that's what he did. He left you alone in a hospital abroad when you were in a coma and then he disappeared. That was heartless. What type of person does that? Even if he had an impulse to leave you, he could have at least reached out to you later and apologized. But he didn't, he didn't even reach out afterwards which means he has no remorse. He did you a favour breaking up with you, you wouldn't want to be with someone like that. I don't want you to be with someone like that."

"Yes, I know. I was heartbroken for a really long time. Because I felt betrayed. One day he was in my life and the next he was gone. I felt I wasn't worthy enough to even receive an explanation from him after all we shared, and I resented him for that. But I don't feel like that anymore. I've chosen to make room in my heart for other things. Resentment didn't serve me anymore, and my heart was full of it. The way I see it, all emotions are sacred. All serve us. Resentment, sadness, despair, or thirst for revenge – all are as good and needed as joy, hope, or excitement are. We need them all, but once they serve us, we need to choose which ones we want to keep inside."

"And now you're doing it."

"Doing what?"

"Speaking like an old professor giving a lecture."

"Don't pull my leg!"

"I do, because you're great, and I'm lucky to have you as my dear friend."

"Don't you think I'm weird?"

"I think you're different, but good-different."

*

That night, just before falling asleep, Alba drifted away again.

She stood on the boardwalk. The fog around impeded her ability to see beyond the wooden planks. She moved forward. First, walking, then, she speeded up. With a strong will to move ahead, she ran faster than she ever had in her life. Then she jumped forward feeling light and held by the winds.

In what felt as a few seconds, she stood barefoot surrounded by giant oak trees covered with English ivy and moss. The light was white and dim. She heard water running in the distance, birds singing softly, and leaves transported by a soft breeze. Leaning on a large granite stone, she crouched down and touched tiny drops of water on top of dry brown leaves. Then she caressed a tiny yellow flower growing on the rounded stone and saw bits of mica and quartz around it.

She took a path. A butterfly with orange wings and blue, green, and violet dots on them fluttered around her. At the meadow, a strong and bright white sunlight received her. In no time, the ground trembled under her feet. Fearless, she gazed to the ground and waited.

Marvelling, she saw a huge reptile like tail twisting among the carpet of dark pink flowers. Amused, she saw a pointed tail with arrow-like emerge among the flowers. The sunlight reflected on it revealing a mix of green, blue, and violet watery colors. It moved up and down. Then, it submerged into the grass carpet again.

When it disappeared, Alba walked back to the path, passed by the large granite stone, looked up, felt light, felt the winds, and stood back on the boardwalk.

Opening her eyes, she arranged the pillow under her head, stretched her arms and legs and sat in bed.

Wow! the pointed tail was so beautiful. Those colors... It looked like a dragon's tail. Was that a dragon's tail?

A NEW BEGINNING

Porto, May 02, 2034.

It's so good to be back again.

Arriving at the Instituto, Alba walked to the operations branch along with her director, Dr. Badeaux, to meet with Dr. Waung and Dr. Luana at the Beehive. Inevitably, seeing the sign of the Biomechatronics xLab name flying around, she thought of Dr. P. Following the letters, she smiled. *I wish him all the best in the Maldives.*

At the Beehive, she listened as the three heads of departments discussed the study about the interaction between M and herself at the hospital. Then, they talked about the policies for deployment of machine workers at the Foundation and also about the way they were programmed to work at the Beehive. The meeting then moved to a discussion about the protocols used to allocate machine workers and to thc need of doing more cross-fertilization among research programs. Alba listened, pleased to be in the meeting with her senior colleagues and, at the same time, looked around searching for M.

After a while, Dr. Luana asked for her thoughts on the best placement for M at the Foundation.

"Well, I don't know how M's performance is here at the Beehive, but based on my experience, I think it could do a very good job supporting patients in the hospital to recover, especially children."

"Please, elaborate further," Dr. Badeaux asked.

"After the surgery to replace the BCI, M brought joy back to me, and that was critical for my recovery."

"Joy?" Dr. Luana asked.

"Yes. As you know, I had a seizure and then surgery. The stay in hospitals, and the surgery, triggered childhood trauma in me related to both. At the same time, I was going through a very difficult personal life situation. I was about to fall into a depression. But I didn't because M helped me bringing joy back into my life."

"Most interesting Dr. Alba. Joy. Most interesting," Dr. Waung said.

"Joy is an excellent ally for healing, that's very true," Dr. Luana added.

"But you experienced joy with M now because you had a bond with M, already, right?" Dr. Badeaux asked.

"That's right."

"So, the bond was important to the experience of joy."

"Yes, I believe so."

"How to create a bond between the patient and the machine worker then?" the director of the Instituto asked.

"Between a child and a machine worker," Dr. Luana clarified.

"Oh, that's easy," Alba responded. M is obsessed with learning. Designed and programmed for learning I mean. We just need to ask the child to teach something to M, that'll create the bond."

"Teaching? Very nice, very nice." Dr. Waung said.

"Perhaps Dr. Badeaux needs a demonstration of your hypothesis Dr. Alba," Dr. Luana said smiling.

"Sure, I can do a demonstration."

"Dr. Waung, would you be so kind to bring machine worker M for a demonstration?"

"I will, very nice."

When M arrived with Dr. Waung, Alba stood up in front of it.

"M! Ready for a lesson my old friend?" she asked.

"Yes, ready."

"So, let's do a bit of a recap from the last session we had when I was at the hospital, okay?"

"Okay."

"M, if you are very, very sad, what do you do?"

"If the level of adversity reaches a threshold of..."

"M, just answer the question please. If you are very very sad, what do you do?"

"I cry."

"And if you have pain, a lot of pain, what do you do?"

"I cry."

"And if you are so so so happy that happiness doesn't fit inside you, what do you do?"

"I'm happy."

"M?"

"I'm happy."

"Come on, we've been through this several times. You cry. If happiness doesn't fit inside you, you cry."

"The affirmation is inconsistent."

"Yes, because we are all inconsistent," Alba said and burst into laughter.

Alba looked at her senior colleagues. Dr. Luana smiled, Dr. Waung giggled and Dr. Badeaux looked approving.

Looking back at M, Alba noticed that the machine had activated its tear device and had a few drops running down its face. As M put its hands over its face to simulate the act of crying, Alba stopped it, "It's okay, don't force it. You'll get there." She burst into laughter again.

"I believe that bonding is easy this way," she told her colleagues.

"I agree with Dr. Alba's idea to deploy M at the hospital. And I propose that Dr. Alba supports as an advisor to implement the program," Dr. Luana said. "Colleagues? Agreed?" she asked.

"Yes, very good, agree," Dr. Waung said.

"Agree. Excellent indeed," the Dr. Badeaux said.

*

On the way out of the data centre, Alba said goodbye to M. "So, it looks like we'll be seeing each other for a while, old friend," she said and caressed its head.

Heading to the exit, she felt happy about the meeting, about being back to work, about the prospects of working with Dr. Luana and M, and about the lightness she felt inside. Then, she thought about her journeys to the mysterious forest again.

It's worth asking.

"M! Listen, remember that I told you about my journeys to a forest and about the oak trees, the moss, the butterflies in the path, the tail. I could use some help here. I can't understand the meaning of it. It's like seeing the pieces of a puzzle but not been able to put it together because I don't have a photo of the full puzzle. I can't figure out the meaning. I only see the pieces in it: the stones are covered in moss, the large butterfly is orange, the strange tail is pointy."

"A pointy tail."

"Yes, there was a pointy tail, in the meadow."

"Pointing where?"

"What do you mean?"

"You said 'pointy'. I ask – pointing where?"

Alba was quiet for a few seconds.

And then, it all made sense. The tail, the shell, the song, all of it.

"Oh, my M, you're a genius. It is pointing somewhere. How didn't I realize earlier?"

"I don't know."

"What? I wasn't asking you. Yes, pointing somewhere. I know where. Thank you, thank you, thank you my friend."

*

Late evening, grateful to the universe for her health, for the developments on her job, for the beautiful place she lived in, for her family, and for her friends, Alba walked to the Praia Da Luz.

Sitting on the sand, she looked up and waited. A crescent moon shone in a dark sky. She knew she was in the right place. At the beach close to the Farol Da Luz.

She listened to the sound of the waves and kept waiting. She knew what she would find there.

And she was ready.

The night was calm, the waves stretched on the shore as in an orchestrated dance.

Then, she heard the song.

Softly first, louder after a while:

'Waves, waves, waves of blue,

coming and going in a dance with you.

Despair and joy, rage, and compassion,

crashing and going in a dance with you.

Waves, waves, waves of blue,

coming and going in a dance with you.

Grief and desire, hope, and bliss,

crashing and going in a dance with you.

Waves, waves, waves of blue,

coming and going in a dance with you.

Flooding and chaos in the order of things.

Tearing of time...

in a wave...

with you.

Waves, waves, waves of blue...'

As the song continued, she sensed Her.

As had happened every time before in Her presence, time and space ceased to exist.

Then, she saw Her facing the ocean. Her robe was suspended in the breeze. Tiny seashells with golden traces adorned it.

A pure white and golden light irradiated from within Her and all around Her.

"You arrived. You found your way back," She said without words.

Alba felt the immensity of the ocean inside her. "I missed you so much," she said, also without words.

"I was always here. Always, waiting for you. You just could not find your way."

"I found you now."

"You found your way back."

In that moment, Alba remembered all the times that, as a child, she had felt Her close.

"They call you many names, now I know."

"Yes, they do."

Alba approached Her and extended her arm to touch her rope. "I call you..." She couldn't finish the sentence because as she looked at her own hand, she noticed that the same pure white and golden light that emanated from Her also emanated from her hand. From her arms, legs, chest, from within herself."

"Now you know. Now you understand," She told Alba.

They continued facing each other for a long while.

"Now you know my dear one, now you know," She repeated.

EPILOGUE: A QUESTION OF FATE

Porto, June 23, 2013.

Dr. Östmann had given very clear instructions about M: move the AI prototype to the Relocation unit 'for destruction'. After weeks trying to figure out what had happened to M, he gave up and moved on. He sent the instructions to destroy M and then he sent his resignation letter to the board. His instructions about M were simple. But as it happens often in life, 'simple', sometimes, becomes 'complicated'.

M arrived at the Relocation unit on a late Thursday afternoon. If it had been any other Thursday afternoon, the facts of this story would have been very different, but it wasn't. It was a special afternoon. And that, affected the way the story of M and Alba unfolded.

At the Relocation unit, in the basement of the operations branch at the Hölfang Foundation, failed AI prototypes were either dismantled (after parts were extracted for re-use in other prototypes) or re-programmed and deployed as machine workers at the Foundation. The infamous E had been reassigned there for deployment at the warehouse, for example.

Matias was in charge of checking in and dispatching failed AI prototypes. Matias was an overqualified intern, who normally completed his tasks efficiently.

M arrived at the unit the afternoon before the celebration of São João, the most important celebration in the city of Porto. Like his colleagues, Matias had planned to leave early to enjoy barbequed sardines and watch the fireworks afterwards. Because he was dining with his soon-to-be in-laws for the first time, he was a bit tense. In an attempt to impress them, he had volunteered to book the restaurant for the evening.

He wanted to impress his in-laws because his girlfriend, Susete, had told him a few weeks ago that her parents 'didn't think much of him'.

"What do you mean they 'don't think much of me?'" he asked her. "Do you mean they don't like me?"

"No, no, it's not that, it's… How can I put it…" she said.

"I have a bachelor's and a master's degree in IT. I speak three languages, well I'm fluent in two but I can speak three. And I have an internship at the Hölfang Foundation, which is a very good first step in my career."

"I know, I know. It's difficult for me to explain it."

"Just tell me, is there anything they don't like about me?"

"Well, it's more my father, not my mother, but also her."

"Umm… So…"

"Please don't be offended. It's your looks."

"My looks? What do you mean?"

"My father said, 'how can a young man wearing a hoodie and sneakers be serious about his professional career?' And my mother said, 'I have to agree with your father… And his hair! He has California highlights – he can't be serious'."

"They don't like me because of my hair? I know what I'll do. I'll impress them. I'll find the best spot to see the fireworks at midnight in São João. With that, they'll be impressed."

But Matias had been distracted during the week participating at a skateboard competition, and only remembered about the dinner and his in-laws in the morning.

When M was brought into the Relocation unit, Matias was busy calling restaurants in Gaia, the city across the river, that allegedly had the best views of the fireworks in Porto. He was failing to book a table for four. All the restaurants were full.

As time passed, he realized that he should have booked the spot at least a week ago, and he got more and more anxious. But it was too late to give up now and he was determined to fight for his love and his dignity until the end.

When M was brought in, he was on the phone checking the eleventh restaurant on his list. He gestured at the co-worker who brought M to place it in the line with other machines. The eleventh restaurant was also full, and his list was over. He decided then to call his girlfriend and tell her that he would go to restaurants in person to try to convince someone to put out an additional table for them. As he called Susete, he scanned M, checked the instructions in the relevant database, and printed a tag for M that he put in a pile of existing tags. It read 'Code D'. 'Code D' meant destruction.

His girlfriend was not supportive. At all. He tried to explain to her all the effort he had put in to finding a table, but she didn't listen. She yelled at him. And ordered him to 'leave everything and run to find a decent place to eat now!'. Like a foot soldier receiving a direct order from an angry general on the battlefield, after she hung up on him, he rushed to the door.

About to exit, he realized he had a bunch of printed tags in his hand that he was supposed to put on the AI prototypes before leaving. Rushing back to the line of machines, he stumbled on his skates, clattered into a few machines, then stood them up again, in a line. He placed the tags on them, and then left.

In the confusion, M received the tag intended for the machine beside it, and that machine received M's tag.

When their tags were later scanned by another overqualified intern, their records were mixed up in the system. In this way, the former star of the eM-M-p was later deployed at the warehouse (as E was), and the prototype that was next in line was dismantled.

So, M's fate changed because an intern in love was having a stressful afternoon trying to impress his in-laws on the day of São João.

Or maybe its fate changed, and with it, the rest of the story, because it was just meant to be.

THE END

Author's note

If you enjoyed *Teaching Machines how To Cry*, please consider posting a review on the site where you purchased it or on another one of your choice. Reviews are a great way to introduce the novel to new readers. Thanks a lot!

Paula